THE BLAKE GHOST

H.P. BAYNE

BAYNE INDEPENDENT PUBLISHING

Cover art by H.P. Bayne with art licensed through depositphotos.com

1

WIND HOWLED OUTSIDE the mall's entrance, kicking up the fresh snowfall and temporarily obscuring the back half of the parking lot.

Sullivan "Sully" Gray pulled up his hood and hunched into his coat, maintaining a rapid shuffle behind his brother, Dez Braddock. At six and a half feet, Dez had the height to move him from one place to the next at a far quicker pace than the average human being. Sully stood a healthy six feet, but if Dez was in a hurry—such as when he was cold and wanting away from the mall as soon as possible—he was impossible to catch.

Dez made it to the SUV first, the engine already running, thanks to the built-in remote start. By the time Sully slid into the passenger seat, the vehicle was partway to warm.

Giving an exaggerated shudder, Dez voiced the obligatory "brrr," then lowered a snow-flaked hood. Sully left his up for the moment, removing hands from his pockets only so he could blow on them.

"Where are your gloves?" Dez asked.

"I think I left them in my SUV."

"Great, Sully. You know it's winter, dummy."

Though Sully didn't turn to witness the eye-roll, he heard it in Dez's tone. He had a retort planned but ditched it as Dez removed his own gloves and dropped them onto Sully's lap.

That was Dez. Sully hadn't been born a Braddock, but it was little more than semantics to the two of them. As far as they were concerned, they were blood. And as far as Sully was concerned, Dez was the best brother in the world. It had been that way when they were kids, and little had changed as adults.

Sully pulled the gloves on, enjoying the warmth inside left behind by Dez's hands. He tucked them beneath the armpits of his coat, holding them there to make the heat last.

Dez reached over Sully and popped the glove compartment, where he placed the small bag from the jewellers they'd just left. After shutting the small door, he pointed from it to Sully.

"Don't let me forget it's in there."

"Says the man who crapped on me for forgetting my gloves."

"I didn't crap on you. Not even close." With his hand on the stick shift, he craned his head left and right, watching for a gap in traffic. Finally, he gave up. "I hate this day."

"It's Christmas Eve tomorrow. Your fault for leaving your shopping until the last minute."

Dez backhanded him in the gut, drawing a combined groan and laugh from Sully. "Hey, I got plenty done beforehand. Eva's ring just wasn't done until today. And Kayleigh wanted that talking fur ball thing. What the hell kind of toy company releases something two days before Christmas, anyway?"

It was true. The electronic toy, whatever it was called, had been released only this morning, bringing a pre-dawn lineup from hell and pandemonium reminiscent of a Black Friday sale as soon as doors opened. Having heard Dez's unfortunate plans for the morning, Sully had tagged along, suspecting his brother's nerves would be frayed from the moment he got up to the second he got home. Sully figured he could both act as calming influence and run interference for Dez while he made for the toy stand. The thought turned out to be unnecessary, with Dez's size working handily in his favour. While other shoppers clawed at each other, no one was fool enough to try swiping a toy from a man as large and angry-looking as Dez.

Even so, the whole episode had left Dez in a foul temper, and the traffic situation wasn't helping.

"Want me to drive?" Sully asked.

Dez paused, ramrod straight, jaw clenched. Finally, all of him seemed to release. "Yeah, go for it."

Sully reluctantly left the vehicle, passing Dez at the rear hatch as they traded spots. Once they were settled back into the SUV, Sully pushed the stick into reverse and turned to watch for coming traffic.

"Two more cars coming," Dez said.

"I see them."

"One the other direction now. Bloody hell, you'd think one of them would want our spot."

Sully gave up for the time being, pushing the stick back into park and eyeing Dez.

"What are you doing?" Dez demanded.

Sully had a question of his own. "What's going on with you?"

"What are you talking about?"

"You've been miserable for the past couple of days—longer, if I'm any judge. I know you hate Christmas shopping, but—" The answer came to him before he finished voicing his previous thought. "Dez."

"What?" Snappish this time, annoyed.

"It's Dad and Aiden, right? You miss them."

Dez glared at him for a long moment. Finally, he responded. “I always miss them, Sully.”

“I know, but it’s Christmas. It’s a bad time of year when you’re missing people. I get it. I feel the same way.”

Dez continued to stare, before finally breaking eye contact and rubbing at the back of his neck. “Every time I see those bloody soft drink or tissue commercials, I want to throw something through the TV.” He sighed. “Look, don’t get me wrong. I’m grateful for Eva and Kayleigh and Mom and you, but yeah, I miss Dad and Aiden. Sometimes I miss them so much it’s hard to breathe. I keep expecting time will make it better, but it doesn’t. Even when things seem to be going good for me, it’ll sneak up and hammer me over the head. And I’m right back to square one, back to how I felt after they died.”

Sully laid a hand on Dez’s shoulder. “I know, D. Same thing happens to me. It’s grief, and it’s natural.”

“I don’t care if it’s natural. I hate it. I want a Christmas like normal people have—with my whole family around me. All of them.”

“Lots of families don’t have the kind of normal you’re talking about. Loss is normal.”

“I don’t care about other families right now, okay? I care about *us*.”

Sully gave Dez’s shoulder a squeeze. “I know we can’t see them. But they’re here, Dez. They’re with us.”

Dez shook his head, a tear dripping down his face, onto his lap. “I used to feel them more. I don’t anymore. Hardly ever. It’s like they’re really gone now.”

Dez’s phone rang through the Bluetooth system, and Sully glanced away long enough to see who was calling. Lachlan’s name showed on the dashboard screen.

Dez heaved a pained sigh. “Come on. Now?”

Sully dropped his hand. “Maybe it’s nothing.”

Dez cleared his throat of lingering emotion, then gave a dry laugh. “When with Lachlan is it ever nothing?”

Several more vehicles were coming behind them, so Sully decided he might as well wait until they’d talked to Lachlan before attempting to back out again. Better to give the call his full attention if, God forbid, it was a job.

“Hey, Lachlan,” Dez said as he answered. “Please, don’t tell me there’s a job. We just cleared the last one, and it’s Christmas.”

“I’m aware, Braddock. I promised you Christmas Eve through Boxing Day off. Today is none of those days.”

Sully met Dez’s eye and shrugged.

“So this is a one-day job, then?” Dez asked.

“Depends on your brother. He there? He’s not answering his phone.”

Sully pulled out his cellphone as Dez replied, “Yeah, he’s here.”

“Sorry, Lachlan,” Sully said. “It was loud in the stores, and I guess I didn’t hear it.”

“Finishing your shopping, huh?”

“Dez was. I got mine done weeks ago.”

Dez shoved him. “Smart ass. What’s the job?”

“Lady called. Wants to see Sully. I think you can guess why. Just go and talk to her, get the ball rolling. If you can’t wrap it today—as I’ve forewarned her—you can get back to it on the twenty-seventh. Got a pen? I’ll give you some details.”

Sully held back a sigh. Anytime anyone wanted to see him specifically, it was because of one thing.

They had a ghost problem.

Sully and Dez worked as private investigators for Lachlan’s firm, though their caseload had changed significantly since

Sully's abilities had made the news a while back. Sully had a unique skill not possessed by most PIs: he could see the ghosts of homicide victims. Lachlan was happy to capitalize on his ability. What Lachlan didn't understand, however, was how it worked.

Ghost jobs weren't like regular ones. You couldn't go out, interview a client, do a little background research and leave things until you could get back to them. If Sully rolled up to a haunting, there was a solid possibility the ghost would recognize in him a chance at help. After that, he'd be plagued by the spirit until he figured out what they needed and got it for them. Show up at the client's now, and Sully might be spending Christmas with his family plus one hanger-on.

Because it didn't do to argue with Lachlan, he kept the thought to himself and dug out a notepad he'd taken to carrying with him when they were working or on call. "Ready when you are," he said.

Lachlan launched into it. "Lady says she and her husband recently built a house, and now they're plagued by a ghost. Her words, not mine. She said they'll wake up in the night to the smell of smoke. They'll search all through the place but won't find anything. It's enough to keep them up worrying, though. They're about to have a baby, so she's very worried."

Sully considered this information. He'd heard of pregnancy sometimes bringing on paranormal activity, although he had no idea why. Sometimes, he imagined, ghosts got as excited about the idea of a coming baby as much as expectant parents did. Or maybe it was the added energy ghosts fed on. Then there was the matter of the new build. Could be if the property itself was haunted, the ghost didn't like whatever had been placed there.

"Did they call the fire department or an electrician or something?" Dez asked. "Maybe there's something burning in the walls they can't see."

"They've called the fire department, and an inspector checked the placed over in detail for hot spots. Nothing. What was interesting, though, was what the fire inspector told them. Apparently, a fire occurred on that very spot nearly twenty years ago. Fatal one too. Three people dead."

Sully's stopped scribbling at "three dead." He knew. Knew without having to ask anything else.

Dez had yet to clue in. "What's the location?"

"McCoy Falls, house on Juniper Crescent, number—"

"Twenty-seven," Sully said.

He felt Dez's eyes on him as Lachlan spat out, "How did you know?"

Sully lowered the notepad to his lap and pinched the spot between his eyes. Tension had built rapidly; a headache would hit him sooner rather than later.

"I used to live there," he said. "It was my last foster home before the Braddocks took me in."

Dez's hand landed on his shoulder. When he next spoke, it wasn't to Sully but to Lachlan. "We can't take the job, boss."

"Jeezus," Lachlan said. "I hadn't even thought about it. I called you right after I—bloody hell. It's the Blakes' address. Of course it is." He heaved a sigh. "Sorry, kid. I didn't think. I'll call and let her know."

"Wait." The word was out of Sully's mouth before he was even fully aware it was coming. He released the bridge of his nose and lifted his head to make himself better heard. "Is that all that's happening? Just the smell?"

"Uh, no. There's more. They're seeing shadows, hearing noises. The lady—Lisa—she's finding scratches and bruises on herself in the morning or after she steps out of the shower. Feels like someone's watching her nearly all the time.

"One of the biggest problems for her is the strain it's causing on their marriage. Her husband doesn't believe in ghosts. He thinks there has to be a logical explanation for the smoky smell, and anything else she's imagining."

"Hard to imagine scratches and bruises," Dez said.

"His explanation is that she's doing it to herself without noticing. She's worried her husband thinks she's crazy or is headed that way. They had a big fight last night. She said she really wants someone to make it stop or, at the very least, to prove she isn't nuts. But we don't need to be the ones to take the job."

"Yes, we do," Sully said.

Dez's hand dropped from his shoulder. "What? Why?"

Sully met his eye, speaking more to him than to Lachlan. "The Blakes are unfinished business for me. I've faced down everything else. The stuff they did, it's never really left me. Anyway, I can't ignore it if they're hurting this woman, if they're targeting her. I've got the power to stop them. I can't ignore that."

"Come on, Sully. Not every problem needs to be fixed by you."

"Well, some problems can't be fixed by anyone else. What if they get some paranormal investigator in there who doesn't do anything but stir up more problems. They need help, and I don't think anyone else can do it."

Dez sighed, his only other response being exactly what Sully expected.

"Goddammit, Sully."

2

McCoy Falls was established before the city of Kimotan Rapids had even existed. Located east of the city, the town was named for a waterfall along the north branch of the Kimotan River.

Many people dreamed about retiring to towns like McCoy Falls. The image of its main street was splashed across tourism pamphlets for the area, and it played host to popular festivals year-round. It's picture-postcard aspect attracted people from all over the country who came to see the falls and stayed for all the other diversions smart community members and town leaders had created over the years.

Everyone loved McCoy Falls.

Everyone except Sully. He'd gone out of his way to avoid it, and he'd pulled it off for nearly twenty years.

That run ended as the town's sign—*McCoy Falls, Est. 1817*—came into view ahead.

Sully cast a quick glance at Dez, reminding himself he wasn't alone. "Hey, D?"

Dez turned and met his eye for the brief time Sully could

manage before having to turn back to the road. Sully added nothing more, didn't even know what he'd meant to say.

It didn't matter. Dez proved he understood him anyway, giving a gentle pat to his leg. "I'm with you, bud."

Sully released a breath, then sucked in another. Not long after he'd gone to stay with the Braddocks, his then-new mom had taken him to see a counsellor upon learning about the abuse he'd suffered in foster care. The counsellor had taught him a breathing technique to use when something triggered memories of what he'd been through. He cycled through it now, using breath to force a calm as he breached the town limits.

While en route, he'd briefly contemplated letting Dez drive but was now grateful he'd stayed behind the wheel. Here, he had some control. He could stop, turn around, keep going. It was in his hands.

He kept going.

The trees, cliffs and old church steeples grew larger as Sully drew nearer. This town had proven homes could be carved anywhere, even into a landscape that railed against it. Good people lived in the wild beauty of McCoy Falls. He knew that, and he clung to it as he tried to suppress the stark knowledge the bad lived here too.

"How you doing?" Dez asked.

With no good way to answer, Sully settled on a shrug.

"This town is kind of a hole, isn't it?"

The words from Dez, spoken at the start of the heavily touristed and charming main street currently awash in tasteful Christmas decorations, had Sully eyeing him.

"I mean, who wants to live like this?" Dez continued. "It looks like something out of one of those cheesy, made-for-TV Christmas movies. I'm waiting for some prissy couple to grab hands and skip down the street with big, dumb grins on their faces."

Dez prattled on about the town, critiquing it endlessly as Sully steered through it. It took only moments to grasp the purpose behind Dez's chatter.

When they were kids, whenever Sully was being tormented by a ghost who wouldn't leave him alone, Dez hadn't only allowed him to crawl into bed next to him. He'd lain there next to him, talking endlessly, telling stories until Sully finally relaxed against his chest and fell asleep. This was Dez finding a way to do the same thing as an adult.

A smile formed as he listened to Dez's voice. He held onto the sound and the feeling until he turned onto the street leading to the site of his former foster home.

Because he had little memory of the area, he'd mapped out his path on his cellphone screen. He would have known Juniper Crescent lay ahead, even without the directions.

A creeping feeling had begun, the sensation he was drawing nearer to something dark. He'd rather face down the ghosts of murderers haunting death row than the Blakes. At least the murderers wouldn't inflict him with anxiety and potential panic attacks.

Beside him, Dez was still chattering. "How much do you think these houses cost? I'll bet no matter what I could save in my lifetime, it would never be enough. And check these Christmas decorations. No way in hell you'll ever find Grinch blowup figures on people's front lawns."

"Eva won't let you put one on your lawn either," Sully reminded him. But Dez's running commentary had served its purpose, Sully's response coming through a smile.

He spotted the sign for Juniper Crescent ahead and skipped the first turn, recalling from the map that he needed to take the second entrance. Dez's conversation stalled out as if he'd noticed and wasn't sure whether he should point it out or not. Before he was able to comment on it, Sully saw the second access point to the crescent and turned right.

The park still stood across the road from the houses here, its image the first thing Sully noted as familiar. He remembered it, all right. Glancing to the right through the windshield, he remembered the first few houses too.

The Blakes had lived in the fourth house from the corner. Sully pulled over in front of the second.

Dez peered at the house next to them. "This isn't twenty-seven."

Sully didn't respond, knowing Dez would figure it out regardless. A moment later, Dez's hand settled on his arm.

"How you doing?"

Again, no good answer. Sully opted for a trip down his dark and unpleasant memory lane instead, his eyes fixed on the park.

"I don't remember much about McCoy Falls, but I remember this place. Sometimes, when Mr. Blake was drinking and I wanted to avoid the inevitable, I'd crawl out my window, walk this street for a few hours. Usually, I'd end up in the park over here. I could see the house, so I could tell when everyone finally went to bed.

"Got pretty good at figuring out the effects of alcohol and how long it would take him to work himself into a rage. When he drank, he drank heavy. I'd give about an hour before he started getting mad, closer to two before he got out of control. I needed to be out of the house before then. Didn't always make it." He gave a small smile, one he didn't feel. "Usually managed though."

Dez didn't say anything.

When Sully turned to meet his eye, Dez's expression registered a combination of anger and pain.

"You never told me much about what happened back then. I mean, I knew about the abuse and everything; you just never really talked about it. And I didn't want to ask."

"I didn't want to talk about it. I knew I was safe with you guys, and that was enough for me. I did all the talking I needed to with the counsellor Mom took me to. She helped me find places to put it."

"We could have helped you too."

Sully couldn't help it. He burst out laughing. "Are you kidding me? Dez, you guys did more than help me. You *saved* me. And not just by taking me in, either. You gave me everything I'd ever needed and never had. I didn't need to sit down and talk out my entire past with you. I wanted a normal kid's life with a family who cared about me and took care of me. You gave me that. Don't think for a second it wasn't enough. It was *everything*."

Dez was an emotional man at the best of times. Before he nodded and turned away, Sully spotted the sheen of tears rimming Dez's lower lashes. Despite that, a smile had formed on his face, letting Sully know he'd managed to say the right thing.

No sense delaying the inevitable any longer. He pushed the stick back into drive and eased his SUV ahead two houses.

The Blakes had lived in a mid-sized bungalow with meticulously trimmed shrubs in front. The old house, left badly damaged by fire, was gone. The house replacing it was a comfortable-looking two-storey, bearing clear signs of a new build. No trees or other shrubs had yet been planted in the front yard to match the other properties on the block, although they seemed to have attempted to make up for it with a trio of white, steel-framed reindeer Sully suspected lit up at sunset. Other decorations made the house appear lived-in, from a string of currently unlit lights rimming the gables to a stylish faux tree on the front veranda to a wreath on the door.

No blowup Grinches here.

When Sully pushed the stick into park and shut off the engine, Dez turned to him. "Can I make one suggestion?"

"Only one? Think you can manage it?"

Dez gave him a mild smack. "Stop calling them Mr. and Mrs. Blake. They don't deserve any show of respect, all right? First names or last. I can't deal with you calling them anything else."

It seemed a fair concession, and one Sully knew he should be making. "Habit, is all. Fine. Jim and Colleen, it is."

"Or Blake and his stupid wife. Can I ask you something?" Dez carried on without awaiting a reply. "Are you really prepared for what could happen if you can't get the Blakes to cross over? You need to bear in mind, man …" He trailed off, and Sully knew Dez didn't want to finish the statement.

Sully did it for him. "They could follow me home after and not leave me alone. Yeah, I know."

"You're still okay to do this?"

"A family needs help, and I need to deal with my past. Anyway, I'm not the scared little kid I used to be. I've faced down a lot in my life, Dez. I know I can handle this. Though I might need a reminder from you at some point."

Dez offered him a smile. "You *can* handle this. I guess I needed to hear you say it. And I'm here for you, Sull, whatever happens."

Sully grinned at Dez, then leaned over him to better study the house. He scanned the windows, searching for faces from the past but saw none.

Not that it meant anything. It could be one or more of the Blakes were trapped inside in death the way they'd been in life.

On the night of the fire all those years ago, Sully had seen Jim Blake's ghost in a frenzy outside the house, eyeing the bodies the fire department carted out. Apparently, he'd gotten no farther. It wasn't unusual for ghosts to be connected to something from life, which acted like a chain they couldn't break. Usually, that was where Sully came in.

"I've never minded the idea of the Blakes being trapped here," he confessed now to Dez. "It's the way they made so many foster kids feel. But it's not fair to the people who live here now. I've forced a ghost to cross over before. Might be I'll need to do that again."

Dez's hand settled on the back of Sully's neck and squeezed gently. "Ready to do this?"

Sully nodded, then led the way from the vehicle.

3

The lady of the house opened the door before they reached it, sticking out her hand with a beaming grin as Sully led the way up the front steps.

"Lisa Everton," she said. "I'm so excited to meet you!"

Lisa seemed young, and Sully put her age at not much above twenty-one or twenty-two. Yet the immensity of her belly revealed she was nearly at the point of responsibility for a new, tiny life.

Sully barely had a chance to meet the handshake when Lisa's face crumpled and she burst into tears. She skipped the handshake and wrapped her arms around Sully's middle. Her belly pressed against him and didn't move, despite the fact the baby had started to kick very near a particularly sensitive spot on his body.

Sully eyed Dez for help but found none there, Dez appearing as uncomfortable as Sully felt. The only thing for it was to let Lisa calm down a little, so Sully uttered a few soothing words while awkwardly rubbing her back.

He struggled to keep his attention on her as the feelings began to hit him. First the eerie sensation they weren't alone, then the smell of booze and cigarettes. Sully peered over the top of Lisa's head, eyes moving slowly through the parts of the interior he could see through the open front door. The day was cloudy, casting shadows inside the house. In one of those shadows, in the deepest corner where a staircase met a wall, Sully saw it.

The shape of a man, features obscured by the dark, but his shoulders and head unmistakably those of Jim Blake. Even from here, the rage bubbling from the ghost clawed at Sully. He'd had nearly twenty years to work himself up, and from what Sully could tell, he'd done a good job of it. Sully couldn't imagine living in this house with this spirit and managing even an hour of sleep.

He suddenly wished they'd arranged to meet Lisa elsewhere. Talking about the Blakes in front of one of them—or more, if the others were here too—wasn't a pleasant thought.

Finally, Lisa hiccuped and released Sully. "I'm sorry. I'm so sorry. I just cried all over your coat."

Sully resisted the urge to swipe at whatever wet patches had been left while Lisa pulled a tissue from the pocket of her sweat-pants and blew her nose. "It's okay. Not a problem."

"This pregnancy thing. My brain is so out of whack. I cry over nothing these days. I didn't used to, I swear."

It seemed the ideal moment to lighten the mood and introduce Dez at the same time. "Hey, I get it. Anyway, Dez cries over nothing too." He turned and grimaced at the glare Dez shot him.

Rolling his eyes at Sully, Dez smiled as he met Lisa's handshake. "Ignore him. I usually do."

Lisa's laugh was closer to a giggle. It promptly stopped as

Dez took the last step up onto the porch, putting himself at full height in front of their much shorter client.

"Wow, you're tall!" she exclaimed.

Dez smirked. "I've noticed. Not much fun going clothes shopping."

She nodded in continued awe, then appeared to snap out of it. "Where are my manners? Come in. I've got the coffee on."

Sully stepped inside first, eyes going immediately back to the corner by the stairs.

The man was gone.

Expecting it wouldn't last long, Sully wanted to take advantage of Blake's absence as soon as possible. He untied and removed his boots next to Dez as Lisa wandered off with directions to come to the kitchen once they were set.

"Anything?" Dez whispered.

"I saw him in the corner by the stairs." Sully nodded with his chin to indicate where. "His personality hasn't changed any."

"Great."

Coats hung on the rack in the entryway, Sully and Dez entered an open-concept living room and kitchen space, the two divided solely by a breakfast bar. Lisa was pouring coffee into cups set before a pair of barstools, so Sully slid onto one while Dez took the other.

Lisa didn't pour herself a coffee, opting instead for a big cup of what looked like water with lemon slices wading inside.

Sully noticed a third, yet-unoccupied bar stool placed at the side of the bar. "Do you want to sit down? Or we could go over to the couch."

She shook her head. "Thanks, but no. Sitting isn't exactly comfortable for me at the moment. There aren't a lot of comfortable positions, to be honest." Another giggle. "These guys better be super-nice to me once they're out."

"They?" Sully asked.

She nodded. "Twins. My husband has a twin brother, and now he's going to have twin sons."

Something in what she'd said sparked a fresh round of tears though she got her emotion under control more quickly this time.

"I'm so sorry. I'm all over the place."

It occurred to Sully this might be pregnancy hormones, but it might be partially connected to something else. Ghosts had the ability to influence people's emotions, sometimes even their physical health.

Another reason he needed to get rid of any Blakes around the place.

"Is your husband home?" Sully asked.

Lisa shook her head. "Ciaran's at work today and does a half-day tomorrow before his holidays. I've been off work for about a month now. My doctor said I need to be careful. It hasn't been the easiest pregnancy."

With Jim Blake around, physically attacking her, Sully had no doubt.

"Why don't you tell us what's going on?" Dez asked.

Lisa took a swig of water, then returned the cup to the countertop before starting. "Ciaran and I got married earlier this year, and I got pregnant something like five minutes later. We hadn't planned on it being so soon. I was on the pill and everything.

"Anyway, Ciaran has a really good job in web design and social media management with some big clients, and I have a good job in IT. We both do well financially, and we were thinking of places we wanted to raise a family. We want our kids to grow up in a smaller community rather than the big city, and both our jobs allow us to work from home quite a bit, so commuting isn't as big a problem. We decided on McCoy Falls."

She paused for another sip of water. This time when she set it down, her hand shook a little. "I've changed my mind. Could we go sit in the living room?"

Sully carried his and Dez's mugs to the coffee table while Dez took Lisa's water and hovered at her side in case she needed a hand. Once she was safely settled in a dining chair she'd clearly placed here—"Easier for me to get out of," she explained —Sully and Dez took spots on the sofa. Then she went back into her story.

"We checked out a few houses, but a lot of them were older and needed a lot of upkeep. With twins on the way, we knew we wouldn't have time for big projects around the house. The easiest thing to ensure our new home ticked all our boxes was to build. We looked around for lots and found this one. It had been empty a long time, we were told. It's near a school and right across from a park. It seemed ideal for a family.

"The build itself had some problems with equipment breaking and tools disappearing. One worker got hurt in an accident. He's okay now, but it was scary. He was working on the second floor and somehow his harness came unclipped, so he fell."

She visibly shuddered. "I would have thought everything was down to the team being kind of sloppy, except for everything that started after we moved in a few weeks ago.

"At first, it was perfect. But within a few days, things started happening. I'd put something down, and it would disappear. I'd walk into the kitchen in the morning to find a smashed glass on the floor. The scariest was finding the big chef's knife sitting in the middle of the island. Even though Ciaran and I don't smoke, we'd smell cigarettes and even alcohol randomly around."

Figured, Sully thought. Not only the fire smell but booze as well. This was Jim Blake, through and through.

"Then things started getting even weirder. We started

smelling something burning, usually in the middle of the night. It got so bad, we called the fire department a couple of times, thinking maybe something was going on with our wiring. But they checked and so did an electrician, and everything was fine. There's other stuff too. Sometimes, I wake up in the morning or get out of the shower and notice big scratches and bruises—and I don't remember doing anything to get them. What's more, they're in places I can't easily reach, like my back. And even worse—" Her voice choked, and she took a moment to regain her composure. "I found bruises on my belly this morning, as if whatever this is, it's trying to hurt my babies now."

Lisa sat back, easing her shirt up a little. Sully's jaw slackened as he eyed the mottling of bruises—not deep or dark, but obvious. Obvious enough to make Sully hate the Blakes even more.

Returning her gaze to Sully, Lisa tugged the hem back down. "This was the last straw, so I called you. I saw you on the news, and I thought maybe you could help me."

She'd said "me," not "us"—a sure sign the couple had been pulled apart over this.

"Lachlan told us you and your husband haven't been on the same page about what's going on," Dez said.

She nodded, and her face scrunched up as further tears threatened, though she sucked this round back. "Ciaran doesn't believe me. He says ghosts don't exist and that's the end of it. He's got an explanation for everything, and the stuff he can't explain he still insists isn't paranormal. The missing stuff he blames on my memory. When stuff gets moved or broken, one of us must be sleepwalking. The smells he says are probably because one of the workers was smoking and drinking around the building material and it's coming out sometimes. The bruises and scratches, I'm somehow doing to myself and not remembering.

"He isn't mean about it or anything. He laughs it off. What he doesn't get is that he's laughing *me* off, as if my opinions and experiences don't count. The first few arguments we had were mostly teasing, but they've gotten worse. He's changing, and I don't like it. I don't like who he's turning into."

This was a new piece of information, and one Sully didn't like either. If Ciaran was changing, it was possible Blake was influencing him—possibly even learning how to possess him.

Sully would need to get Blake out of here one way or another.

"What I really don't understand is the way the neighbours look at us," Lisa continued. "Especially this older lady next door. She smiles and everything, but it reminds me of the way you react to someone when they've been diagnosed with a terminal disease, like people feel sorry for us. I mean, do they know the place is haunted?"

"I don't think that's exactly it," Sully said. He had a choice to make: tell Lisa the truth or spare her another stress and hope she never found out.

Yet if the neighbour knew something about the past, it was only a matter of time before she, or one of the others, told Lisa. Better it came from Sully since he could be both sensitive and tactful about it.

Even so …

"How sure are you that you want the answers?"

Lisa's eyes flashed open a little. "You know, don't you? You know what's in my house."

"If I tell you, will it help you, or will it make it worse?"

"Can you get rid of it?"

Sully would allow nothing else. "I won't quit until I do."

She nodded and sat up as straight as her unborn children would allow her. "Then tell me. Knowing is better than wondering. Whatever it is, I can handle it."

He sure hoped so. "First, I need to disclose some backstory. I used to live here—in the original house, I mean. I was in the foster system, and the couple who lived on this property took in foster kids."

This time, Sully was the one receiving the sympathetic gaze. "Were they nice?"

Once again, he debated between truth and lie. In the end, she'd asked for the truth. Giving her anything else would feel wrong. He shook his head. "Jim Blake, my foster father, was an alcoholic. He got mean when he drank."

"Mean how?" Lisa almost whispered it, as if uncertain whether asking was okay.

Sully had no problem telling her, not anymore. "He was physically abusive. His wife, Colleen, looked the other way. They had a son called Jimmy. When I knew him, he was sixteen or seventeen. He wasn't any better than his father, only I was told he did worse with the girls."

Lisa's face had taken on an intensely sad expression as he'd talked. "I'm so sorry. That's horrible." She turned to Dez. "Were you there too?"

He shook his head. "Sully came to live with my family after the Blakes. After …" He trailed off, eyeing Sully.

Sully again opted for truth, picking up where Dez left off. "After a fire killed the Blakes. I'd imagine that's why the lot was empty all this time. The property's history isn't very nice."

One of Lisa's hands shot to her mouth. "Oh my God. Oh my God, are you serious? A fire?"

"It was an arson," Sully said. "Another foster kid who used to live here. She was abused and was really messed up over it."

Sully didn't go further down that road, his own, more recent experience with the woman one he wished he could forget.

"The burning smell, it's because of that, isn't it? They're trying to set fire to my house."

Though Sully had considered it, he thought there might be a more innocent explanation. "If the fire department couldn't find heat in your walls, I doubt that's the problem. The smell is probably connected to the Blakes."

"But what you said about them, it explains my injuries, right?"

Sully nodded slowly, with regret. "Yeah, I think it does. People who are jerks in life don't stop being jerks when they're dead." Boy, did he know firsthand.

The statement had sparked something, a heaviness he suspected would lead to something more. He hated having Lisa around here if Jim was about to have a meltdown.

"Lisa, are you able to go somewhere for a couple of hours?" Sully asked. "I'm going to have to deal with this, and it might get worse before it gets better. I don't want you around for it."

"Ciaran would be upset if he knew I left the house with strangers." Even as she said it, she sounded hopeful, as if praying one of them could convince to her do exactly as Sully had suggested.

Dez fielded her concern. "We're licensed and required to get updated criminal record checks done. You can trust us to take care of the place. And Sully's right. If things start happening, better you're not around."

Lisa was convinced, as evidenced by her heaving herself out of the chair and making for the front door. There, she stepped into slip-on boots and grabbed her coat. From a shelf, she retrieved her purse and car keys. With assurances they would call once it was over, she left.

Dez stood in the living room, watching through the window as Lisa backed out of the driveway and drove away. “So what’s the deal, Sully? Are things about to start happening?”

Sully stood in the centre of the room and focused. The energy was heavier, stronger—if he could slap a word on it, angrier.

“Oh, yeah,” he said. “Things are about to happen, all right.”

4

THE FIRST THING Sully wanted to do was to figure out how many entities he had to deal with.

As he'd expected, Dez didn't like the sound of that. "You mean, they might all be here?"

"Maybe. Hard to tell with Blake's energy coming in so strong. He was always overpowering. It's possible I can't sense anything else because he's pushed himself so far forward."

In Sully's case, it wouldn't matter. Even if Colleen and Jimmy were lost to him in feeling, if they were indeed here, he'd see them eventually.

To seek them out, he fell back on memory.

"Whenever Blake was about to fly into a rage, Colleen and Jimmy went to their rooms and stayed there."

"And that's what you're feeling? An oncoming rage?" Dez asked. "I mean, I can feel something too, kind of. It's heavy in here, almost hard to breathe."

Sully had been visually searching the room. Now he turned to meet Dez's eye. "That's him. Once we put an end to this, the place will feel a lot different."

Sully headed for the stairs, turning to make sure Dez was with him before making any attempt to head up. Though determined to face this down, he wasn't stupid enough to think doing it alone was a good idea. He'd been there, done that, and had nearly lost his life more than once because of it.

Dez had been a police officer. It took guts to walk into a dangerous situation. Having a partner with you didn't make you any less brave; it made you less likely to get your head shot off.

Even if Blake's spirit wasn't in control of any firearms, he was dangerous enough all on his own and in his own way. If Sully had learned anything about dealing with malevolent spirits, it was that cockiness came before the fall.

"You doing okay?" Dez asked.

Sully nodded and turned back to the stairs. "Yeah. Just stay with me."

"Every step, Sull."

Sully managed a grateful smile before heading up.

The lower floor had been on the chilly side, which Sully had put down to the season and to the fact a woman carrying the extra weight Lisa was might choose to keep the heat down. But when he reached the upper floor, it felt almost as bad as stepping outside.

"Did they leave a window open or something?" Dez asked.

Sully shook his head. "I think it's Blake."

"I don't get it. It's like one massive cold spot."

"I think he's sucking energy from the place."

Dez didn't answer immediately, and when Sully turned to see why, he discovered Dez had gone stock-still, eyes wide. "He's going to pull some poltergeist shit, isn't he?"

"I think he's going to try. If he's able to move objects from one place to the next and cause injuries to Lisa, he's not helpless."

One of the bitter pills about the paranormal world was that negative emotions, like anger and fear, most often gave the strongest boost to ghosts. Sully hadn't encountered many happy poltergeists in his life. Fortunately, he came with power all his own—one he'd learned to use over time.

Dez knew it. "You going to do your whole reverse possession thing?"

Sully tipped his head as he listened to the silence around them. "I'd rather not. The idea of sucking in that man's energy isn't my idea of a good time."

Even so, the possibility was there if he needed it.

Deciding they'd stood here long enough, Sully led the way down the hall to a set of double doors that had to belong to the master bedroom. No sign of any spirits in here, nor did he find any in the nursery, ready to go right across the hall.

"Anything?" Dez asked.

"Good news is I don't see or sense Colleen or Jimmy anywhere."

"So you think they crossed over already?"

"They must have."

Dez tilted his head. "So why not Blake? Why'd he stick around if his family left?"

"Maybe he's scared to go because he thinks he won't be going anywhere good."

"Yeah, okay, but given what you told me about them, wouldn't they be scared to go too?"

Sully considered the thought. "Jimmy was young. Could be he hadn't grasped how bad it was, the stuff he did. And Colleen, much as I hated the way she never helped me or anyone else, I guess I can kind of see another possibility now. Maybe when Blake wasn't beating the foster kids, he was beating her or

Jimmy. If so, we were an outlet for him, making her safer. I guess I can't blame her for that."

Dez crossed his arms. "Yeah, well, my sympathy remains at level zero. Lady could have called and reported him. God knows you had the injuries to prove what you'd been through. If she'd said something, they would have shut him down and removed all of you."

"And who's to say where we would have ended up? Dez, some of my injuries came from those other homes. Blake wasn't the only one to abuse the kids in his care." Sully faced Dez fully. "I don't regret anything, okay? If I hadn't been where I was the night of the fire, I wouldn't have met Dad. I wouldn't have ended up coming to live with you guys. There's a reason for everything. You don't have to like it, and I love that you're pissed off for me, bro, but I've mainly come to terms with my past."

Dez held his eye for a few long seconds. His face didn't soften. "Sorry, Sull. I'm proud of you for being big enough to forgive the bastards, but I'm not. I remember what you were like when you came to us, how scared you were, how uncertain of yourself. They made you that way. All of them. I'm not about to let that go."

No point arguing, so Sully settled for patting Dez on his outermost crossed arm.

Dez seemed to take the gesture as his cue to let loose, shouting loud enough to be heard in the deepest corners of the house. "You hear me, you prick? You think you're a big man, hurting women and kids? Huh? Let's see what you've got! Come at me, asshole!"

Sully gave Dez a shove. "Dez, quit it! What the hell are you doing?"

"You're trying to find him, aren't you?"

"I want him targeting me, not you."

Dez glared down at Sully. "Tough. Not happening. He's targeted you enough for one lifetime. Now he's going to deal with me."

Something showed behind Dez, and Sully shifted to see the ghost of Jim Blake standing, glaring at Dez. But something else showed in his face.

Focus.

Thoughts of Lisa and Ciaran came to Sully, the thought of Ciaran being influenced or even partially possessed Blake.

Now it seemed the spirit's target had transferred.

Sully grasped Dez's arms. "Dez, listen to me. This anger, it's not all yours."

"Like hell."

"It's not. I need you to take a breath and try to relax. Focus on me, all right? We're going to walk out of here, go take a break or something."

"I'm not leaving, not until I deal with that asshole! Quit fucking arguing with me!" Dez's voice shook with rage. A bad sign.

"You can't. Not like this. You and Blake, you're feeding off each other, okay? You have to—" He stopped abruptly as another glance to the side revealed no further sign of Blake. For a moment, Sully relaxed. The air was warmer, the atmosphere in the hallway lighter, as if the house had been successfully exorcised.

Then it occurred to him. The reason Blake wasn't in the house anymore was because he'd gone somewhere else.

Dez.

Sully turned his eyes back up to his brother's face. "Oh shit."

Dez's face, but not. This Dez's expression was dark, twisted. Furious.

Worse, it was directed at Sully.

"You know your problem?" Dez snarled. "You're weak. You've always been weak. I protected you, always did, still do."

"Dez, this isn't you. I need you to—"

"You know what? Fuck you. You don't like the way I deal with shit, you handle it. I'm gone."

It dawned on Sully what Dez meant. He was going to leave —and unwittingly take Blake with him.

As Dez turned toward the stairs, Sully stepped in front of him. "You can't leave. We need to deal with this."

Dez shoved Sully aside. "Go to hell."

Sully grabbed Dez's nearest arm—his left. Unfortunately, this kept his dominant right free to take a swing.

And he did. A good one.

The blow caught Sully on the side of the head, spinning and dropping him all in the same motion. He lay there, head reeling, and opened his eyes to a swirling image of Dez looming over him. Sully sensed the assault coming, and he struggled to crawl away, at least far enough he could try to climb to his feet.

Dez—or rather, Blake—wasn't allowing it.

Only he didn't hit him again. Dez's large, solid hands shot out and clamped around Sully's throat. Dez said nothing more, voice given over to furious grunts Sully recognized not as his brother's but his once-foster father's. Fighting for breath as he clawed at Dez's hands, Sully could get nothing past the fingers compressing his windpipe. When Blake shook him, Sully's oxygen-starved brain flashed back to a time when he was seven, to this exact scenario. His throat in Blake's grip, head whipping back and forth as he was shaken like a rag doll.

He'd barely escaped death that day. He wasn't going to be as lucky today.

Attempts to break Dez's grip having failed, his body and

brain edging dangerously close to unconsciousness, he did the only thing he could think of. He went limp.

It didn't help. Blake kept squeezing, kept shaking him.

Desperation faded as unconsciousness enveloped him.

5

Consciousness returned slowly, a piece at a time.

The sensation of something solid beneath his body. The smell of fresh carpet. A sound of a door slamming, the rumble of an engine.

Sully pried open one eye, waiting a few seconds for the ceiling above him to quit whirling before he opened the other.

His throat hurt, and he rubbed at it a moment before forcing himself to sitting. Though his head spun for a few seconds, and the change in position led to a throbbing in his head, he kept himself upright.

He wasn't dead, which he was grateful for. But that was it.

Dez was gone. And the dangerous ghost of Jim Blake had gone with him.

Sully propped himself up on one arm, using the opposite hand to pat himself down for his cellphone. It was where he'd placed it, in the pocket of his hoodie, and he pulled it free.

He stared at it, deciding best to break this to Eva. Finally, he gave up searching for the right words and dialled. No correct way for telling someone her husband had been possessed by an evil spirit.

"Everything okay?" Eva asked upon answering.

Sully's response was immediate. "Why?"

"Because Dez texted me a while ago, telling me you guys were headed to McCoy Falls. He said you were going to meet a client at the house you used to live in."

Eva knew about Sully's childhood. Her concern was for him right now, not Dez.

Boy, was she in for a surprise.

"Not the same house," Sully corrected weakly. "Same property. The house was destroyed."

"Okay, so how's it going?"

"Uh, not so good." Sully leaned up against the nearest wall and massaged at the ache in his neck. "Dez kind of attacked me."

A pause. "What do you mean, he attacked you?"

"He choked me out. Right out. I mean, it wasn't him. It *isn't* him. He's not himself right now. I need to warn you, in case he comes back to your place. Maybe you and Kayleigh should go somewhere else for a while, just until I can find him and sort this out."

"Hold on. What are you talking about?" Controlled worry laced her voice, the kind born of a decade in policing.

Taking a breath, Sully pulled himself to his feet. He'd need to make sure Dez was gone rather than somewhere in the house arming himself and preparing to finish the job. He headed carefully down the stairs, explaining the situation to Eva on the way.

"Where is he now?" she asked as Sully reached the front door.

"I don't know. His coat and boots are gone." Sully peered out a tall, thin window to the side of the door. His heart sank. "And so is the SUV."

"Yours or ours?"

"Yours. He picked me up this morning."

"Okay. Okay, that's good. The vehicle's equipped with a GPS system. I've got an app to help me track it. Give me a sec."

Sully stepped into his boots and laced them up while he waited on Eva, wondering why he even bothered. He had no vehicle, after all, and no immediate way to get into the city from here.

"I've got an address," Eva said. She groaned. "Liquor store. Sounds about right for the man you described. God, it's bad enough Dez being possessed. I don't want him drinking and driving besides. What if he hurts someone?"

"Where's the liquor store?"

"Main Street. Stay where you are. I'm coming."

Sully pulled on his coat while balancing the phone between his jaw and shoulder. "No way. I need to find him. I'm heading over to Main. Meet me there."

"Watch yourself, all right? He's already attacked you once. Don't give him another chance."

"What choice do I have? It's Dez."

Eva sighed. "Be careful, all right? I need to drop Kayleigh off at a friend's place before I come out there. Keep me posted."

They disconnected, and Sully dropped the phone into the front pocket of his coat. Then he zipped it up, ensured the knob lock was on, and ran out the door.

During the sprint to Main Street, Sully put in a quick, breathless call to Lisa, warning her against going home yet. Until he was certain Blake wasn't taking Dez back to the house, he didn't want to risk their heavily pregnant client being in the way.

"When can I go home?" she asked.

Sully huffed out a reply. "Give me a few minutes. I'll get back to you about that. Which way is the liquor store once I hit Main?"

"What? Why?"

"Trust me. Which way?"

"If you're coming from Christopher, it's left."

Sully checked, relieved to see the sign for Christopher Avenue. He paused for a quick breather, realizing he'd need to pass along a more detailed warning. "Thank you. And, hey, if you see Dez anywhere, don't try to talk to him, all right? What you said the ghost was doing to Ciaran, he's doing now to Dez. I need to find him and deal with it."

"Are you saying he's *possessed*?"

An admission Sully didn't want to make about Dez with a relative stranger, but he also had a job to do. Right now, job one was protecting his client.

"Yeah, that's what I'm saying. Avoid your house for now. And avoid Dez, whatever you do. Okay?"

"Sure, yeah, of course. I'm at a friend's. I can stay here a while."

"And Ciaran? He won't be back from work for a bit yet?"

"No. He texted a few minutes ago, and he's having a busy day. Oh my God, he can't find out about this. If he knows I went to you with this, he'll really think I'm crazy."

"One thing I can say with some certainty is if Ciaran started acting like a jerk after you moved in, it's not his fault. I'm going to fix this. I'll get back to you once I do."

He didn't wait on a response, simply disconnected and got back to his run.

It hadn't felt this far when they'd driven to Juniper Crescent, the time seeming to blink past when Sully had wanted it to crawl. Now, covering the distance on foot and with a crisis on his hands, Sully couldn't reach his destination fast enough.

By this point, Dez—operating under the influence of Jim Blake—might have already left the liquor store, but Sully was hoping he'd spend some time there. His recollection of Blake had him pegged as a whiskey man, enjoying his rye neat or mixed with soda, depending on his mood. The liquor store would have been reorganized at some point over the years, but Blake would figure out quickly where to find his preferred drink. By the time Sully arrived at the store, Blake would probably be long gone.

Sully stopped running, allowing himself both a breath and a think. Blake had always followed the same routine on his drinking nights. He'd pick up a bottle after work, come home, and tuck into it. First his "wind-down" drink. Then his "supper" drink. After that, he'd stop bothering to name them.

One thing the drinks had in common was each one was tipped back in the same location.

At home.

Sully placed his hands on his knees as he bent at the waist and focused on drawing deeper breaths. The freezing air made it impossible, with anything more than shallow inhales bringing on a round of coughing. But he'd have to catch his breath before returning to the house. He'd put six or seven blocks between himself and the property, and while he was in good shape, running in winter wasn't an easy matter. And he'd need to be ready to do battle with Blake—and Dez—once he got there.

Another thought hit him. He'd locked the door before he left, and he didn't have a key. Nor, for that matter, did Dez. Not that Dez couldn't kick the door in if he wanted inside badly enough, but it could prove a barrier Blake might not cross. It wasn't, after all, his house. Not anymore.

Which led to another problem. It might bode well for Lisa and Ciaran if Blake didn't feel at home in the new house, possibly preventing his return now he had a set of wheels and a meat suit to ride in. What it didn't do was help Sully. If Blake chose not to return to the house, he'd have to decide where else to go. And despite having once lived with the man, Sully knew next to nothing about him.

He called Eva.

"On my way," she said in greeting. "Anything your end?"

"No. I was running for the Main Street, but I don't think I'll get to the liquor store in time. You mentioned the GPS. Can you see where he is now?"

"Hang on." A moment of silence suggested Eva was checking. "He's still at the liquor store."

Answer enough for Sully to get back to running. "Stay on the line with me and tell me if the vehicle leaves."

"How far away are you from the store?"

"Few blocks." A few long blocks. A thought occurred to him, and he puffed out the observation. "Dez used his cash."

"What?"

"Shopping. Used his cash for stocking stuff."

Eva was quiet a moment. "And if this Blake guy's in control, he'll have to rely on Dez's cards. And he won't know the PINs. That's what you're thinking, right?"

"Yeah." Which was only a happy thought if Blake wasn't so desperate for a drink he resorted to something illegal, like shoplifting or robbery. Dez's PI licence had been granted on the knowledge he had no criminal record. And good luck explaining to a judge you weren't guilty because you'd been possessed by a ghost at the time.

Sully was less than a block away from Main Street when Eva supplied more bad news.

"Sully, he's moving. Heading west on Main."

Sully picked up the pace, ignoring his screaming lungs, pounding heart and aching legs as he closed the remaining distance. Someone ahead hadn't shovelled their sidewalk, and he skirted it, dashing onto the street. He slipped on the compacted, icy snow but caught himself.

Just in time to see Dez's SUV cross Christopher Avenue. And keep going.

"Just saw the SUV," he said, panting. "Went past on Main. Don't think he's going back to the house."

Sully made it to Main Street, head whipping to the right as he strained to see where Dez's vehicle had gone. He thought he could make it out in the distance, continuing west.

"Eva?"

"He's heading out of town, I think," she said. "Any idea where Blake would be going?"

The answer did nothing to settle Sully's heart rate.

"No," he said.

6

WITH NO CHANCE of catching up to Dez on foot, Sully forced himself to think through how best to handle this.

"Think like an investigator, you idiot," he muttered. Easier said than done as he stood there, panicked, watching the SUV—and Dez—disappear into the distance.

Having disconnected with Eva, he returned to his former posture, hands on knees as he struggled for a full breath. Light-headed and nauseated, for a moment he thought he might need to sit down. Instead, he closed his eyes and focused on settling his nerves. His thumping heart was as much caused by dread as the run. Dealing with the emotional cause would help him handle the physical.

He took in what air he could, forcing his mind past the events of the past ten or fifteen minutes so he could decide what to do now. It occurred to him the first thing he could do was to head to the liquor store. There, he could suss out whether Blake had managed to get himself a bottle—and if he'd done anything illegal in the process.

Sully covered one block before spotting the liquor store on

the next one, tucked in next to an antique shop. Situated as it was, the liquor store had managed the improbable task of appearing quaint, a wolf in sheep's clothing given what Sully's life had taught him about alcohol. One of the consequences of time spent with people like Blake was that Sully could count on one hand the number of times he'd allowed himself more than a couple of drinks. He'd been drunk twice in his life and had hated the feeling, the sensation of being out of control. Another consequence of his past was the fact he couldn't trust easily. Putting himself in a position of being vulnerable to others was something to be avoided.

Beyond that, alcohol stifled his control over his psychic ability. With a weakened capacity for putting up his usual walls, the wrong ghosts could slip through. For some reason, darker spirits seemed to find him when he was at his weakest.

All good reasons to avoid booze. Consequently, Sully had visited a liquor store only a few times in his life, and always to buy gifts for other people.

He didn't think they'd ask for ID unless he went to the till, but he made sure he had his driver's licence at the ready, anyway. Then he headed inside.

As the parking situation on the street might have suggested, the place was a flurry of activity. It seemed a few people had taken the day off. Either that, or they had skipped out from work to try to stock up on the Christmas alcohol before the after-work rush began. Consequently, it had created a during-work rush. The one person working behind the till had a five-customer lineup. Needing info soon, Sully peered around the store for someone else who could help.

Nerves as fraught as they were, he jumped as someone touched his elbow and spoke loudly next to him.

"Can I help you find something?"

Sully turned to see a bespectacled older woman staring up at him, apologetic smile on her face.

"Sorry to startle you," she said before he had time to answer.

"It's okay. I wanted to ask about someone who came in here, actually. Really big guy, red hair. Did you see him?"

Her smile fell away. "Yes, and I was about to call the police about him."

Damn. "What did he do?"

"He stole a bottle of rye. One of the expensive ones too."

Sully grimaced. "A twenty-six?"

She nodded.

Double damn. Dez was a big guy, so he could pack away a little more alcohol than others before it hit him, but he wasn't a big drinker either. The last thing Sully wanted was to go toe-to-toe with a violently drunk Blake while he was using Dez's line-backer-like body.

Of course, it seemed he had a more immediate problem. "So he stole it?"

She shrugged. "Well, he *tried* to pay, I guess. He couldn't get his cards to work. Couldn't remember his PINs. He gave my clerk what he had in his wallet, but it wasn't enough. He grumbled something about us getting the money later and took the bottle before she had a chance to stop him. I've been debating whether to call police or not. Given his attitude, I'm highly doubtful he intends to return."

On his way there, Sully had considered how he would handle such a situation, should he arrive to find one. As a result, he had a reply ready. "Listen, that guy is my brother, and he's having a really tough time right now. If I pay what he owes, will you keep the police out of this? I'm going to find him and talk to him. I have no doubt he'll be back to apologize once he's himself again."

The woman's frown lessened. "Well, of course, if the outstanding bill is paid, I won't be so concerned."

Sully pulled out his wallet and checked his bills. Definitely should be enough there. "And no one else will call?"

"I'm the manager. The job falls to me. No one will call."

"Thank you. How much was left on the bill?"

"Twenty-seven and change."

Sully plucked out a twenty and a ten and handed it over. "Keep the change as an inconvenience tax."

The frown disappeared altogether, replaced by another grin. "You're a much nicer young man than your brother."

"Maybe today," Sully said. "He's usually not like this."

The understatement of the year.

"Did he happen to say anything else before he left?" Sully asked. "Anything about where he might be going?"

"I asked my clerk, as it happens. It's the sort of information police might be interested in knowing. But no. He didn't say anything else besides the whole money-later thing. Wasn't a very talkative fellow."

Definitely not typical Dez.

With nothing else to ask, he thanked the manager more profusely for her understanding and headed back outside.

It occurred to him he should call their boss to report what had happened. Lachlan would be pissed if he only found out about it because Dez got arrested somewhere. Best to get on top of this now.

"So how's the job?" Lachlan asked. "You doing okay there?"

"Uh, not exactly." Sully explained the situation, leaving nothing out. When he finished, he was met with a wall of silence so long, he checked his phone screen to ensure the call hadn't been dropped. "Lachlan?"

"I'm here. I was waiting in the hopes you were going to add a 'just kidding' to the end of your story."

"I wish. Eva's on the way to get me, and I just paid off Dez's—or should I say, Blake's—bill. Problem is, I wouldn't put it past him to drink in the car. If he gets stopped with open liquor—or worse, causes an accident while drinking and driving—it'll be a disaster."

"And you said the SUV's equipped with GPS?"

"Yeah."

"I can't believe I'm about to say this out loud. Any chance the dead guy will know how to disable the tracking system?"

"You can do that?"

"If you know where to look. Good thing, I guess, is the guy croaked nearly two decades ago. GPS in vehicles wasn't a big thing yet. Chances are he won't even clue in."

A good point, one Sully was relieved to concede. "Thanks, Lachlan."

"What can I do from my end?"

Sully reached the intersection of Christopher Avenue and checked both ways before crossing the road. "Nothing. Eva and I will work with the GPS for now, to track him down. If we run into trouble, I'll let you know. Whatever happens, I have a feeling I'm the only one who'll be able to deal with him once we find him."

"Any idea how you're going to manage that?"

"Not exactly. I'm thinking I should be able to draw Blake out of Dez easily enough, providing I'm able to focus. I didn't get a chance back at the house."

"Fine, but what then? I don't think this guy's going to turn out to be one of your ghosts who skips happily into the light once you sort out his problems."

Sully gave the street ahead another long scan, hoping to see Dez's SUV. Nothing. "I don't think so either. I'll have to find another way."

"Such as?"

Another answer Sully didn't want to voice. "No idea."

7

Sully covered the length of Main Street by the time Eva arrived to pick him up.

She called as she entered town limits, allowing them to coordinate a location to meet. When at last Sully hopped into the passenger seat of Eva's car, he was frozen, his toes beginning to lose feeling inside his boots and his teeth chattering.

Eva cranked the heat up full while Sully eyed himself in the visor mirror. His facial hair, ordinarily a couple of shades darker than his hair, was pure white around his nose and mouth, frosted over from breath.

"Have you been able to check on the SUV recently?" Sully asked, voice shivering with the rest of him as he held his hands near the vents.

"Periodically. We'd better check again. He wasn't far from here the last time I looked, but it's been a few minutes."

Eva picked up her phone and leaned toward Sully so they both could see the screen. Sully noted a dot on the screen he assumed represented Dez.

"Where is this?" Sully asked.

Used her forefinger and thumb, Eva expanded the map and pointed to a spot toward the top. "This is roughly where we are, on the outskirts of McCoy Falls." The blue dot was northwest of their location, not nearly as far as Sully would have expected.

"I thought he'd have been a lot farther away by now," he said.

"I think he's stopped. The vehicle hasn't moved since the last time I checked." She tilted her head and narrowed her eyes at her phone. "That's got to be a grid road near him. He's probably a couple of miles off the highway. But I can't see anything else around there."

"Only one way we're going to find out."

Eva signalled her agreement by handing her phone to Sully, shifting into drive and cutting a U-turn. The engine revved hard as she raced down the highway, eating up the distance between them and Dez.

"What are you going to do once we get there?" Eva asked.

"Whatever I can do. I need to pull Blake out of Dez."

"And then what? Won't he just get back in?"

"He'll try. I'll have to hold him."

Sully felt Eva's eyes on him and he met her gaze before she had to turn back to the road.

"What?" he asked.

"The only way you can hold this Blake guy is by doing that reverse possession thing you do, right? Are you sure that's a good idea?"

Sully wasn't sure at all, if he were to be honest with himself and Eva. He'd done it before, and successfully, not long ago. But that entity had been more or less friendly with him. Blake would be different. He would fight, and hard. Enraged and drunk on the power he already held, he would be filled with anger and hate and darkness.

All the negative emotions would feed the dark part of Sully's soul and risk his turning into the same thing Blake already was. Though he'd successfully controlled that part of himself in the past, he'd also fallen deeply under its power. His corralling it had so far been down to the better nature of the spirits he'd taken in or had come at the end of a hard-won battle. He'd always come back, but it wasn't always easy.

And people he loved had gotten hurt because of it.

"Sully?"

He turned, again meeting her eye. She held his gaze a moment before returning her focus to the road—long enough he read the doubt there.

"I know, okay?" he said.

"I have complete faith in you," she said. "You know I do. But this is different. This man controlling Dez, he's not like other ghosts you've dealt with. You have a history with him. A bad one."

Sully dropped his gaze to his lap. "Yeah."

"He was abusive, right?"

Sully nodded.

"You were just a little kid. I've been around a lot of people on the job who were abused as kids. That kind of fear and pain, it doesn't just go away. You've found a place to put it where you can live your life without it constantly hanging over you, but it's a part of you. It's a part of who you are, and I think it's a big part of why you're so dedicated to helping others who are hurting. You've made it a strength, Sully, but with Blake, it's still a weakness. He knows your buttons because he's pushed them all before."

"I'm older now. I'm not that kid. Not anymore."

Eva didn't say anything, not right away. The silence lay heavy with things not yet said.

He waited.

Finally, she spoke. "I've never told you this. When I was a kid, my mom dated this guy for a while. It wasn't long after my dad died, so she was kind of a wreck. She really struggled with not having a man around, so this guy moved in seemingly five minutes after they met. One night, he came into my room."

Sully froze, eyes widening as they fixed on Eva.

"I won't get into the rest of it, other than to say my mom came in before things went really far. But it was bad enough. I got really screwed up because of it. Luckily, my mom, messed up as she was back then, was a bear about her kids. She kicked him out and called the police. He was charged and eventually convicted, and he served time in jail for it. And Mom got me in with a great counsellor. I was able to put all the pain and shame someplace where I could get on with my life. A big part of why I went into policing is probably down to what happened to me, so I could help others who went through it, I guess."

She glanced at Sully. "As strong as I feel now, as far as I've come, some things still put me right back there. I know you're the same. Dez has talked to me about it, when you've had a bad time about something and he doesn't know how to help. With the experiences we've had, we've got triggers, and there's no trigger as bad as seeing the people who hurt us.

"I saw the man again a couple of years ago. He was at a bar we needed to attend to make an arrest on an outstanding warrant. I saw him, and I suddenly felt about five years old. Just like that. If it wasn't for Dez's support that night—"

Her voice cracked, and Sully's stomach dropped for a second time since he'd gotten into the vehicle. Eva rarely cried. When she did, it was a big deal.

He reached over, laying a hand on her shoulder until she'd

regained control. Before he could remove his hand, she clasped his fingers in hers.

"What I'm trying to say," she said, "is we have soft spots inside ourselves we need to acknowledge. If you take that man's energy inside yourself—even for a reason as noble as protecting your brother—you risk falling under the weight of it. If you do, if you become something dark, you might end up doing some really bad damage. Not just to yourself, but to us. There's got to be another way. If this were any other spirit, Sully, I'd know you could handle it. But not this one. Please, don't try."

She gave his fingers a last squeeze before releasing him. He eased out the air in his lungs, mind spinning with everything Eva had told him and everything he no longer had the answers for. There was nothing he wouldn't do for Dez, including facing down the most horrible moments of his life. But Eva had spoken a truth he felt deeply inside himself. He was risking unlocking a door he needed to keep shut. If he opened it, he wouldn't be saving Dez—he might end up hurting him worse than Blake ever could.

Sully pinched at the corners of his eyes, desperation drawing tears.

"I need to make a call," he said.

"To who?"

"Marc. Maybe he'll have an idea about what I can do." Marc Echoles, a friend who worked as a professor of Occult Studies at the university. Though he didn't always have the answers, he could often point Sully in the right direction. And right now, he needed direction.

So did Eva, Sully realized. "You need to make the next right. That's the grid Dez turned down."

Sully placed Eva's cellphone onto the centre console where

she could see it and pulled out his own handset to make the call. Marc's cellphone rang once before he picked up.

Check that. His voicemail picked up.

Sully swore quietly and disconnected without leaving a message.

"Probably away for the holidays," Eva suggested.

Sully shook his head. "It's his cellphone."

"Probably busy for the holidays, then." She offered an attempt at an encouraging smile, not quite passing it off. "I guess we'll have to figure this one out ourselves. Or is there someone else you can call up to help us out?"

Sully's first thought was of Raiya Everton, a practicing Wiccan with some incredible skills and knowledge all her own.

Then he thought of someone else. Someone who wasn't quite a someone so much as a something.

"Ghost train," he whispered.

He felt Eva's eyes on him without the need to turn. "What?" Her voice was sharp.

"The ghost train. Remember? The Edge Creek Light. There's a reaper on the train. If I can pull Blake out of Dez, the reaper can take it from there." Sully finally faced Eva, hope rekindled inside him, a possible solution at his fingertips. "If we can get Dez and Blake to Edge Creek, the reaper there should be able to help."

Eva lost a shade of colour. Only then did Sully recall what had happened the last time she'd been out there.

"Eva—"

"It's okay. It's to save Dez. It's okay."

He touched her shoulder again, then withdrew his hand. She had her own demons, having been forced to fatally shoot a man who was trying to kill Sully.

"Once we get there, you can stay in the car, no problem," he said. "I can take it the rest of the way."

"One thing at a time," she said. "For now, let's focus on finding Dez, all right?"

Sully nodded. One thing at a time was right. Anything more would be beyond what he could deal with.

8

THEY DROVE for what felt like a long time down the grid, their progress slowed by icy patches and recent snowdrifts fingering across the road.

A set of tire tracks backed up the GPS data, telling them they were on the right path.

"Shouldn't be far now," Sully said. "Looks like he's a short distance off the road." He squinted and zoomed in a little more. "Hang on. Nope, there's a second road. I think he turned onto it and stopped there."

He watched the unmoving GPS tracker as Eva navigated their rough path, telling her to slow even more as they neared the second road, currently hidden behind a row of evergreens.

"Should be somewhere behind those trees, I think."

Eva reached the spot—indeed a road—and stopped.

Sure enough, the SUV sat there, parked haphazardly on the roadway, the piled snow making driving impossible.

Eva pulled onto the approach, enough to get her vehicle off the main road, then turned off the engine and pulled the keys. "If

I try to drive in there, I won't be getting out without a tow truck."

"I don't think Dez will either," Sully said. "Looks like he's stuck."

"I can't imagine anyone uses this road anymore. It probably hasn't been ploughed all winter. If it wasn't for the ditches, I wouldn't even know it was here."

Sully met her eye. "Ready?"

"Gonna have to be. Let's go."

They stepped out of the car, Sully reluctantly leaving the heat behind. Nothing good awaited them out here, and he wasn't looking forward to whatever lay ahead. But he wanted to get Dez out of this as soon as possible, so he set a brisk pace toward the SUV.

Eva jogged around her car to catch up. "Do you see him inside?"

Sully shook his head. "Not yet. But we're still a bit far."

He worked on fixing that, walking as quickly as the snow allowed until he reached the vehicle.

No Dez.

"Crap," he muttered.

Eva moved past him, head bent to scan the ground around the vehicle. Meanwhile, Sully checked the SUV doors. Locked. Just as well, since Eva's expensive Christmas gift and Kayleigh's hard-to-get toy were likely still inside.

Eva spoke from a short distance away, drawing Sully's attention to the roadway behind the SUV. "He left footprints." One gloved index finger extended toward the road until Sully gained her side. "You can see them here, in the middle of his tire tracks. He went back the way he came. Come on."

Sully maintained as fast a pace as he could, jogging back toward the road while keeping his eyes on Dez's footsteps. Back at Eva's car, they scanned the area, searching the world of white for any specks of black on the horizon that might be Dez. Nothing revealed itself. Nor did similar bootprints show up immediately, plenty of tire tracks having flattened the snow in many places. For the moment, they left the car where it was, scanning the snow for clues, spreading out in either direction when their initial search came in empty.

Finally, Sully picked out a print matching those seen on the unploughed road. "Eva! Got something over here!"

She jogged over, lending her own assessment. "Good job. Looks as if he's headed north. Come on."

She led the way at a run back to the car, leaving Sully to bring up the rear.

"Hold on," he called out. "Why don't we keep walking it? If we're driving, we might miss something or drive over a clue."

"We still need the car," she said. "If he doesn't want to come willingly, it'll be a hell of a lot harder for us to drag him all the way back here."

"Point taken. I'll walk while you drive. I'd hate to miss something."

Eva nodded. "Let me walk it though. Working with the police, I've tracked more than my fair share of suspects using footprints. It's second nature. Get in and follow. And keep checking the surrounding area for Dez. If you keep your eyes up and I keep mine down, hopefully we can get this sorted out sooner rather than later."

In the driver's seat, Sully crawled along the road behind Eva, scanning the area around them. They continued for what felt like forever, Eva moving at a jog at times but otherwise maintaining a slower pace, head turned toward the ground. Sully had shut off the radio partway along, the merry Christmas platitudes doing nothing for his stress level. Doubtful Burl Ives or Bing Crosby had ever been in the position of locating a missing brother who'd been possessed by an evil spirit the day before Christmas Eve. Just as well too. This wasn't the sort of thing Sully would wish on anyone.

At last, Eva jogged back to the vehicle, face red from cold as she dropped into the passenger seat. "Holy hell, it's freezing out there."

"You still have his trail?"

"Yeah, and he's been holding a steady path since he got stuck. I need a warm-up, but no point losing time. Keep driving ahead—go slowly. Watch for any paths off the road."

Her teeth chattered lightly, so Sully cranked up the heat while he drove. He didn't voice the thought he suspected they both shared: Blake probably wouldn't notice the cold—a fact that could prove fatal to Dez.

Five minutes turned into ten, ten to twenty. Still nothing to signify and end to the seemingly endless situation.

At last, the land evened into a long, flat stretch, allowing them to see for a good mile in each direction. No Dez anywhere in sight, but something else revealed itself.

"Looks like a yard site up ahead," Eva said. She turned to Sully. "Let's get there. I'm willing to bet Blake noticed the same thing."

Sully pressed down on the gas, clearing the distance to the farm. As they neared, Sully could tell it was an operating farm. A herd of cattle stood in a large pen near a barn, and smoke billowed in a thin cloud suggestive of a chimney. Sure enough, Sully steered into the yard to find a newer SUV parked next to the side door of a comfortable-looking bungalow. Christmas decorations were up. A set of wire-mesh reindeer bent as if to munch at snow in the yard in front of the house, and a large plastic Santa adorned the front step, while a row of icicle lights dangled from the eaves. Snowflake shapes had been placed in the windows, suggesting the interior was likewise decorated.

Sully pulled up behind the SUV and led the way from the car.

"What if he's here?" Sully muttered to Eva on the way to the side door. "Blake didn't react too well to me the last time."

"Let me take the lead," Eva said. "I still want you close by in case something goes wrong. I can't imagine a situation in which Blake agrees to come quietly, not if he's got his own agenda. I hate to say it, but we might have to fight him."

"I hate for you to say it too," Sully said.

With no way to predict how the situation would unfold, Sully took the wooden steps to the side door. No doorbell in sight, he rapped, then stepped to the side to place Eva in direct sight of the door.

A few seconds passed before the sound of movement from inside reached Sully's ears. Eva pasted on a warm smile, and Sully did the same. He was relieved when the woman whose face appeared in the doorway met their grins with her own.

"Yes?"

"I'm sorry to disturb you, ma'am," Eva said. "We're looking for a friend of ours. We wondered if he might have come this way. He's very tall and—"

"Red hair?" the woman cut in.

Sully and Eva each nodded enthusiastically.

"That's him," Eva said. "Is he here?"

"He was. He got stuck on the road, not too far from the highway."

"Where did he go?"

"Oh, well, he was hoping for a tow, but my husband is replacing a tire on the frontend loader today. He's got another hour or two of work to do. Your friend—Jim?—didn't want to wait. He seemed in a rush to leave."

Sully didn't doubt it. Even now, Blake might be under the impression he'd killed Sully earlier today. Last thing he'd want was to stick around anywhere long enough to give the police a chance to catch up to him. Of course, he could simply jump out of Dez's body anytime he wanted and leave Dez holding the bag.

Or could he? Maybe it wasn't as easy to get out as in, like climbing out of a deep river with strong currents. Even if he could get out easily, why would he want to give up Dez's body? He was young, strong and solid—everything a bully like Blake would yearn to be. He'd have to search long and hard to find another human being as big and as powerful as Dez.

The lady hadn't quite answered the question, so Eva asked again. "Do you know where he went?"

"Not precisely. My husband offered to give him a lift into town, though. They must be there by now, as long as the roads weren't bad."

"McCoy Falls?" Eva asked.

The woman shook her head. "Kimotan Rapids."

Sully's heart dropped. If Blake disappeared into the expanse of the city, it might be next to impossible to locate him. "Is there any way you could contact your husband and ask where he dropped Jim off?" he asked.

"He doesn't often answer his cellphone, I'm afraid. He hates technology. I can ask him when he gets back?" Her voice rose in a question.

Eva smiled. "I'd really appreciate it. If you have someplace to jot it down, I'll leave you my cellphone number."

"Of course. Step inside for a moment while I get a pen and paper."

As the woman headed farther inside the house, Sully gladly

stepped into the entryway, pushing the door shut behind Eva to seal in the warmth. His relief was short-lived, his thoughts instilling in him a whole other kind of chill. His brain spun through scenarios, all the things that could happen before he was able to pull Blake from Dez.

Eva turned and waved him toward her. He leaned over, allowing her to whisper to him. "Do you think the man Dez is with is in any danger?"

Sully gave it some thought before shaking his head. "Blake could be plenty charming with adults when it suited him. It was the kids in his care who had reason to worry."

"But you're an adult now, and he went off on you. And he was going after the people living on his old property."

"They were intruders to him. As for me, I was a threat to him, and he knew it. It was pretty obvious I was there to remove him from the place. The guy who's driving him around now is doing him a service. He has no reason to hurt him."

At least, Sully hoped not. Fact was, years had passed since Blake had been separated from his body. Time did things to ghosts, same as it did to living people. Being trapped in a single location, alone and with nothing but dark memories to occupy oneself—that would do something to a spirit. Blake's family was gone and he was alone. He probably carried with him the knowledge someone had made it happen. He'd be traumatized, he'd be furious and he'd be paranoid—a bad combination at the best of times. Add booze to the mix, as it seemed Blake was eager to do, and you ended up with a powder keg primed to blow.

When the lady returned with a small notepad and a pen, she jotted down the number Eva gave her. Sully provided his, in case; then, he and Eva both took out their phones and keyed in the woman's number and her name—Brenda—saving it in their contacts.

"We really appreciate this," Eva said.

"You're very welcome. He seemed quite stressed. I mean, anyone would be after getting stuck and having to walk several miles in the cold. But I had a feeling there was something more. I felt bad for him. I think my husband did too."

Sully and Eva thanked her one last time. After receiving another promise Brenda would call once she spoke with her husband—Keith—they left.

For a while, they drove in silence, Eva back behind the wheel. Sully finally turned to her, mouth opening to speak, but he promptly shut it. Though she wasn't crying, her face was tight and hard, her hand clenching the wheel hard enough to impede circulation.

"You okay?" he asked.

"Fine."

"Eva."

Her body seemed to sink, shoulders dropping, spine softening, facial muscles changing her expression from hardened to worried. "I guess I was really hoping he was there. Every minute he's under that bastard's control is time he might do something he shouldn't. Or he might get hurt. I mean, he's already done some really bad stuff. What's to stop him doing worse?"

Sully could think of nothing to say in response—he couldn't argue the point, not given what had happened earlier. He settled for the next best thing, laying a hand on her shoulder.

He left it there until the skyline of Kimotan Rapids came into view through the windshield.

9

THEY HAD GONE AS FAR as they could—for now, anyway.

Eva pulled into a truck stop on the city's northeastern limits and parked so they faced the highway. Sully headed inside to hunt for snacks but couldn't find anything he thought he could stomach. He settled on a couple of bottles of soda, paid and returned to the vehicle.

Eva was on the phone.

"Thank you so much," she said, then disconnected.

Sully closed the passenger-side door behind himself and stared at her. "Please tell me that was Brenda."

She nodded as she tapped at her screen, bringing up the map function. "Brenda said her husband made a stop at a house in the city, but Jim came back to the vehicle after speaking to someone at the door. He was pretty upset afterward and asked to be taken to another location, this time outside the city. Keith said the road Jim wanted him to turn onto was all snowed in, so he couldn't get through. Jim said he'd walk and got out. Keith left him there. Brenda said Keith was pretty spooked and was glad to be rid of him. Something felt off. He was thinking of calling the police so was relieved to find out we were searching for him."

"Do we have a location?"

"City address was twelve-oh-four Sycamore. She gave me rough directions to the rural spot, based on what she was able to get from Keith."

Sully placed the pop bottles into the centre console cupholders and put on his seatbelt. When he was set, Eva handed her phone to him.

"See if you can narrow it down," Eva said as she reversed out of their spot. "He said it was roughly twenty kilometres southwest, just off Highway Twelve."

That came as a relief to some extent. Edge Creek was to the south of the city, meaning they'd have less distance to travel with a combative Blake than if they picked him up to the north or west of the city.

Sully played with the map until he was able to get a rough idea as to distance. A small town was close to the twenty-kilometre mark on the highway in question.

"Did Keith mention anything about passing through a small town?" Sully asked.

Eva shook her head. "I asked about any towns or landmarks. Brenda said he hadn't mentioned anything. She'll get back to me if she hears otherwise."

"So I'm thinking he dropped Dez off is a little bit north of Phillip's Point. Unfortunately, I'm not seeing a road there."

"If it's snowed in, it hasn't been ploughed, so it's possible it's not counted as a proper road," Eva said. "I'm thinking farm access. See if you can find a map of the rural municipality. Might be we can figure it out based on who owns property around there."

Using his own phone, Sully went on an internet search, first needing to figure out the name of the RM in question, and then changing pages to search for a map. He found one on the RM association's website and zoomed in once he'd downloaded it onto his phone.

His heart thudded as he located the supposed drop-off area. "Hey, Eva?"

She met his eye briefly before turning back to the road, brows lifted. "What?"

"There is an old road there, and like you thought, it leads toward a farmyard. The farm and the land around it are owned by someone named Cecilia Blake."

Eva's brows lifted further. "Obviously a relative, then. See if you can find an obit that will tell us who she is to Jim Blake."

"Already on it." The most obvious place to look was the obituary for Jim himself, but too much time had passed. If the obit had ever been online, it was long gone.

What he did find was an obituary naming Jim and his family as pre-deceased to another Blake, this one named Walter. Jim was listed as Walter's son. Cecilia was a daughter.

Sully passed along this latest info to Eva, then turned to the Kimotan Rapids address on Sycamore. Nothing immediately came up. Given more time, a property search would be an option, but time wasn't something they had a whole lot of at the moment.

Lachlan might have some contacts in that area who could speed up the process. He put in a call to his boss.

"About time you called," Lachlan grumbled. "I was going to try you again right away, anyway. You find him yet?"

"No, but we're following up a lead. We talked to the wife of someone who gave Dez a lift into KR and then to a rural location where he left him."

"In the middle of winter? This place heated?"

"No idea, but I doubt it. Given the road was snowed in, I'm guessing it's an abandoned farm."

Lachlan's lips made a flapping noise as he exhaled noisily. "You boys don't know how to do anything the easy way, do you? What do you need?"

"Help filling in a blank. Twelve-oh-four Sycamore Street. It was the first city address Blake asked for. He came away from there in a bad mood. We're guessing it used to belong to a family member, particularly given the rural location he's at now is still owned by a Cecilia Blake. According to an obit, she's Blake's sister. Can you find out?"

"On it," Lachlan said. "Keep me posted, huh? More regularly, I mean." He hung up, and Sully turned to Eva to fill her in.

"Lachlan's going to check into who owns the Sycamore Street place."

Eva shrugged. "Probably doesn't matter a whole lot right now. I'd be willing to bet, like you said, it either does or did belong to a family member of Blake's. Probably the latter, given he didn't spend longer than a few seconds there and came away in a mood."

"A lot has changed since he died. It's got to be one hell of a shock to find out how much."

"The bigger question, I guess, is what he expects to find at the old farm."

Sully nodded. "And what he'll do when he finds out it's not what he remembers."

Years as a police officer meant Eva knew the quicker routes through a city busy with end-of-day traffic. Even so, they got held up at a couple of spots nearer the city centre before they were able to access the freeway that would take them around the city.

Lachlan phoned back as Eva navigated off the freeway and onto Highway Twelve.

Sully put Lachlan onto speaker in time to catch what he was saying. "I got the results back on the property search you asked about. Twelve-oh-four Sycamore belongs to a Christine Pierce, no relation whatsoever to the Blakes. She bought it six years ago and has lived there since. I found what you were really after in the sale records. Seller was none other than Cecilia Blake."

"Awesome, Lachlan, thanks," Sully said. "We'll dig up some info on her, just in case."

"No need. Already did it."

Sully grinned. "Of course, you did."

"Right after she sold the house, she moved to a supported living setting. She's only middle-aged, but she's lost her eyesight. Kitson Place is the facility. Unit fourteen is hers. Independent living, with someone coming by each day to check on the residents to make sure they're okay and get their meds. Got a pen? A phone number was listed for her on the documents I found. Looks like a cellphone to me."

Sully opened his notes app instead. "Go ahead."

Lachlan rattled off a series of numbers, and Sully repeated them back at him to be certain he'd thumbed them in right.

Certain he had the correct number, Sully smiled warmly into his phone. "Thanks, Lachlan. We appreciate the help."

"Listen, kid, I may be a grumpy old bastard, but I care about that numbskull brother of yours too, all right? Get him back. And call me as soon as you do."

He disconnected without waiting on a response.

"What should we do about Cecilia?" Sully asked. "I mean, is it worth talking to her before we go after Blake?"

"I want to get to Dez ASAP. But the more info we have about Blake, the better. See if you can reach her while we're en route."

Sully tapped the number into his keypad and listened to the ringing. Three sounded before a voice came on the line.

"Hello?"

The voice sounded friendly enough, the one word questioning and warm rather than snappish. With any luck, if this was indeed Cecilia Blake, the apple had fallen very far from the family tree.

"Is this Cecilia Blake?" Sully asked.

"It is."

"My name is Sullivan Gray. You don't know me but—"

"A Sullivan Gray once stayed with my brother and his family. Might that be you, by chance?"

This was unexpected. Sully didn't remember any extended family stopping by the Blakes' while he'd lived there. Then again, it was a long time ago. Some memories could have been lost to time.

Unfortunately, the bad ones remained exactly where they'd always been.

"Yes, that's right," he said. "Do you remember me?"

"I never met you. I do know about you though. You were living there at the time of the fire. The police spoke to me right after and asked about you and another boy who lived there, Brennan Wakeman. I wrote the names down, thinking maybe one of you started the fire. Of course, this was before we learned the truth about the girl who actually did it."

"I'm sorry about what happened to your family," Sully said.

Cecilia chuckled. "No, you're not."

It seemed a strange thing to hear from a voice as kind as hers. "I'm sorry?"

"The investigation revealed more than details of the arson, you know. You boys were badly beaten. And the girl—Margaret—she suffered even worse. I attended the hearings in court. I wanted to know why it happened. At first, I didn't want to believe the things Jim and his son did, but finally I could no longer deny it. So I don't want to hear your apologies. I should be apologizing to you."

It took a moment for a reply to form in Sully's brain, another second or two to voice it. "It's okay. None of it was your fault."

"I should have been checking in on Jim and his family. If I had, I would have seen something was amiss. But I hid my head in the sand. I didn't want anything to do with my family, and you paid the price. You know, sometimes I think my physical blindness is God's way of punishing me for turning a blind eye to my family's sins."

Sully suddenly wished he was able to have this conversation in person. "It's not your fault, Cecilia. It really isn't. Anyway, as bad as things were, something good came out of it for me. The man who took me in after was a police officer I met while I was being questioned about the fire. He and his family became my family, and they're the best people I've ever known."

"I'm so glad to hear that." And she was. Her tone made the statement true.

Before calling, Sully had thought of the reason he'd give as to why he was reaching out now. Though it wouldn't exactly be factual, but this was one of those times a white lie might be a blessing. He couldn't picture anyone being pleased to hear their deceased family member was still floating around and had learned the art of possession.

Before he had a chance to broach the topic, she spoke again. "Are Jim and his family still hanging around?"

"Uh—" Not a question he expected.

"I listened to most of the news coverage of your uncle's trial, you know. I thought you must be the same Sullivan Gray who had lived with my brother's family. Once I heard the name, I listened to stories about the case every day afterward. You can see ghosts. That's what they said in the news."

"Uh, yeah, I can."

"And are they? Still around, I mean?"

Truth it was, then. "I haven't seen the others, but Jim was stuck at the old property in McCoy Falls."

"Was? He isn't now?"

God, how to explain this. Sully pinched at the bridge of his nose and gave himself a couple of seconds to get his head screwed on before answering. "Spirits can attach themselves to things—usually houses, sometimes objects too—things that held meaning for them." A pause. "And sometimes, they can attach to people."

"Is he attached to you now?"

"Not me. My brother. And the problem is, Jim's really strong. It's pretty common for ghosts to influence the living. They can make people feel sick or stressed or emotional or drained. Really strong ones can do even more. They can make people do things. Sometimes they can even take over someone's body."

"Like possession?"

"I know it's a lot to take in."

"Not for me. I've always been very interested in the paranormal. As for Jim, I long ago accepted what kind of person he was. I very much believe him capable of bullying his way into anything, even with him dead. What can I help you with?"

Sully exchanged a glance with Eva. She wouldn't be able to hear the other end of the conversation, but he wanted to let her know things were going better than he expected.

"My sister-in-law and I are trying to find my brother. His name's Dez. I think Jim is trying to get someplace meaningful to him. We have information a Good Samaritan dropped him off at some property you own. I think he was trying to find you."

"Which property is this?"

"Initially, he asked to be taken to a house in KR on Sycamore Street."

"I haven't lived there for six years."

"We know. Any idea why he'd go there?"

"Not to look for me, I don't think. We had little to do with each other. If he came by my old house in the city, it was to beg a ride, nothing more."

"That might make sense. When he saw you weren't there, he asked the guy driving him to take him southwest of the city to some land that shows you as the owner. The driver left him, and we're heading there now to try to find him. You know what land I mean?"

"Oh, yes. It's a farm you're talking about—you're right, it means something to him. It's where we grew up."

Sully shifted in his seat, the seatbelt stopping him from leaning forward as much as he would have otherwise. "Does anyone live around there?"

"No. The old farmhouse is still there, but it's been abandoned for years. My father willed me the land after he passed away a few years ago. I sold two of the quarters and I'm renting the others until I can get a good price for them. The sooner I can sell the place, the better."

Sully raised a brow. "Why?"

"Put it this way—Jim came by his behaviour honestly. Our

father was a hard man. Mom died young—and I'm not entirely convinced my father didn't have a hand in it. After that, our father went completely off the rails. He'd always been an awful person, but he started drinking heavily, and all the anger he carried, he took out on us. We suffered routine beatings, both of us. It's really no wonder Jim turned out as he did. Doesn't make it right, how he treated you and the other kids, but it gives an explanation.

"Jim hated our father as much as I did. If he's going back there now, it isn't to catch up with a loved one. It's for revenge."

"Why now?" Sully asked. "Why not while they were both still alive?"

"Dad was a large man, very strong after years of farm work. Jim was built more like Mom—short and on the pudgy side. He was never overly strong, which became a source of tension between him and Dad. Dad wanted a big, strapping son who would take over the farm. Jim had no interest, and realistically couldn't have managed it even if he'd wanted to."

All the time Sully had spent with the Blakes, he'd never once thought of Jim as short, pudgy or weak. To Sully as a seven-year-old, Jim had been monstrous in proportions, a huge man with the strength of an army.

Only he hadn't. He'd been something beyond what Sully's perceptions suggested. Like Sully, Jim had suffered at the hands of an adult he should have been able to trust. The difference was, Sully had found a way out. Jim hadn't.

And now Jim had found himself a new body, one that was everything his father had wanted him to be. Jim hoped, Sully believed, to turn the tables on his father, once and for all. What he'd do once he learned he couldn't was anyone's guess.

"I'm sorry about what you went through," Sully said. "No kid should have to experience those things."

"You're right about that. But this is why I should have figured out what kind of foster father Jim would be. I turned a blind eye, Sullivan, and I'm sorry. If there's anything I can do to help you now, just name it."

Sully let his smile show through his reply. "You've already done it."

10

THE FARMYARD WAS some distance off the highway, far enough to cause Sully a new worry.

As Eva pulled onto the approach to what must have once been the road to the farm, Sully turned to her.

"It'll be a long way to lug Dez if Blake won't come willingly."

Eva's eyes didn't leave the scene out the windshield—snow-covered fields, a grove of evergreens and oak in the distance and a set of footprints leading away from the highway.

"I know," she said. "We'll just have to do the best we can. It's for Dez."

Good enough for Sully.

They exited the vehicle and followed Dez's trail through the knee-deep snow. Sully belatedly realized he should contact Lisa and gave her a call.

"What's going on?" she asked immediately upon answering.

"We've got a handle on him," Sully said. "Don't worry. I won't let him near you again, no matter what. You're safe to go back to the house."

"Good, because I'm actually already there. Ciaran called saying he was on his way home. I needed to make sure everything looked the same as it did when he left. I don't want him to know anyone was here. It would be too hard to explain."

"I understand. I'm sorry if anything was messed up. We kind of left in a hurry."

"I get it. Thanks for what you've done already. Will you let me know when it's officially over and that you guys are okay?"

"Of course," Sully said. "I'll be in touch sometime this evening."

He disconnected and refocused on their current task.

A five-minute walk became ten, their path often impeded by deep snowdrifts.

The sun was setting as the two-storey brick house came into view, peeking from around the trees. Its style suggested it had been built in the nineteen twenties or thirties, and the look of the place told Sully someone had been taking care of it until sometime within the past decade. Not anymore, though. Staggered two-by-fours barricaded the lower floor windows, and the shingles were peeling away, leaving the roof sinking with rot in one spot this side.

A few more steps and they had a better glimpse of what must have once been a very comfortable farmhouse. A veranda ran the length of the front, and a small balcony had been built over it, opening out from one of the upstairs rooms. Tiny windows beneath the gables suggested a usable attic space, although the basement—if one existed—didn't boast any windows or access points.

Eva tugged Sully toward the trees. "Let's hold here a minute and watch. We don't know what we're walking into."

Though Sully was eager to move, Eva was a trained police

officer. If she wanted to scope out the situation for a minute, she had her reasons. He stood next to her and waited.

"No board over the front door," she observed. "He must have pried it off. If all the windows have been boarded up, the door probably was too."

True. "Guess we'll have to go the same way."

"What I'm trying to decide is whether there might be any firearms or other weapons inside. I'm sure Cecilia would have removed any guns after her father's death, but the land's rented out. Do you see any signs the farmyard is used by anyone on a regular basis? Any outbuildings look newer? Quonsets or shops?"

Sully scanned the area as Eva did. "Nope. Just one run-down barn and a few smaller buildings that look as old as the house."

Eva nodded. "That's what I'm seeing too." She met Sully's eye and offered an encouraging smile. "Guess there's no way to know what we're facing if we don't go in there, huh?"

Sully shook his head, saying nothing, and waited for Eva to make a move. Finally, she stepped from behind the tree and started toward the house.

Sully stayed at her side but took the lead as they reached the veranda.

He studied the snow-covered steps. Bootprints, one wooden stair snapped in the middle beneath someone's weight.

Yeah, Dez had been here, all right.

"One set of prints going in," Eva said. "Unless he went out the back, he should still be inside."

That might be a comforting thought. Or it might not, depending on what they were about to find.

Sully stepped cautiously over the broken stair and climbed onto the veranda. The wood creaked beneath his weight but held.

"Guess there's no way to sneak up on him, huh?" he said as

Eva's approach behind him made the same noise.

She grimaced but said nothing.

Sully turned back to the door. He drew in a deep breath and released it before grasping the knob and turning slowly.

His mind flashed to the household items he and Eva had discussed between the trees and the house, ones that could potentially act as weapons—knives, fireplace implements, gardening tools. Though guns were quicker and more efficient, makeshift weapons could be equally as deadly. In Jim Blake's hands, anything could be a serious problem.

Sully stepped inside.

Unchecked weather damage had left the floors in the inner porch rotting and worn. Best he could tell, using the light filtering in from outside the open door, the brick walls and largely protected windows on this floor had kept out the worst of the damage. Nonetheless, several winters without heat had taken their toll.

He checked over his shoulder. Once they entered the house more fully, they'd be left with only what light the spaces between the boards on the windows would provide.

"Do you hear anything?" Eva's voice was a whisper in his ear.

He shook his head. Nor did he see anything to suggest where Dez might be. A dull glow came from the top of the stairs before them. Even from this vantage point, a couple of the stairs appeared ready to collapse. No way Dez could have made it up there without crashing through.

He had to be close.

Sully settled his nerves and took another step inside.

Clear of the interior porch, he saw more light ahead and to the right—as if someone had pried off a board or two at the back of the house as well.

Damn.

Sully pointed for Eva's benefit, but her eyes had already found the same thing.

"Let's go," she suggested from the back of his right shoulder. "Could be he saw us coming and took off out the back."

The thought got Sully moving. The temperatures both in the house and out were well below freezing. Jim Blake couldn't die twice, but Dez had been forced to spend a lot of time outdoors already.

The lit room ahead proved to be a kitchen, the cupboards visible through the doorway still in good shape. Sully stood there a moment, this side of the open door, listening. No sound—no creaking floors, no rustle of clothing, no breathing—reached his ears. Sully feared Blake had already taken Dez somewhere else.

He stepped through the doorway. And stopped dead.

Across the room, next to a dusty table, stood Dez, partially empty bottle of whiskey open next to him.

For a moment—a fleeting couple of seconds—Sully caught a glimpse of Dez, his mouth opening to exhale, brows lifting above his eyes' inner corners.

Relief.

It was gone almost as soon as it had come.

And so was Dez.

Narrowed eyes now fixed on Sully, quiet yet heated appraisal. Searching for weakness.

"You. I thought I dealt with you." Dez's voice but not, grating and hateful with none of his warmth.

"Not quite," Sully said.

He stepped forward as Eva pressed on his shoulder to move him. Dez's eyes tracked to the newcomer. For a moment, his brows again shifted upward and his lips twitched.

Recognition.

Dez was still in there, near the surface. Close enough to know what was happening. Close enough to experience the horror of knowing he had no control.

In a flash, the light in his face was gone.

"Hi, Dez," Eva said.

"I'm not Dez."

Sully took a few more steps forward. Far enough to spot an iron fireplace poker clutched in Dez's left hand.

Left hand. Blake had been left-handed.

Sully stopped. Eva, in his peripheral vision, circled to the other side of the room, putting up a front should Blake attempt to go through them.

"Who the hell are you?" Blake growled, eyes boring into Sully's. "I know you."

"You don't remember? I thought maybe you'd figured it out back at the house."

Blake hefted the poker in Dez's hand. "Don't screw with me. Who are you?"

"I was your foster kid for a while."

"I had lots of foster kids."

"Sullivan Gray."

Eyes flashed open at the name. He remembered. "You. You were there. The fire. My family. *You.*"

Blake let loose a wail and charged, fireplace poker raised. The move was quick, far quicker than Sully had anticipated. He ducked at the last second, the air raking his hair as the tool sailed over his head.

A blur of Eva slammed into Dez's back as the momentum from the swing turned him. Sully lent his own body weight to the restraint attempt, pressing Dez against the counter while stretching for the poker to disarm him.

Blake howled and exploded, shoving off from the counter

and forcing Sully and Eva back. Lashing out lightning-fast with his right hand, he caught Eva on the side of the head and sent her flying into the side of the table.

Sully cried out her name, then realized distracted focus was a major error. Blake grabbed him, lifting and propelling him backward until he hit hard against a wall. Sully's lungs rattled with the impact, drawing a gasp. No time to give in to pain, Sully pushed at Dez's chest, intending to slip away from him.

Blake didn't budge.

He backhanded Sully hard across the side of the head, snapping his head to the side. Before Sully could recover, a solid, cold and heavy weight pressed against his throat. Twisting his head a little, he saw the poker clutched in both Dez's hands, a weapon for Blake to pin Sully to the wall by his throat. Dez's green eyes blazed with a hate unnatural to them as he hefted the poker—and Sully's body with it.

With his throat compressed beneath Dez's weight, breathing was impossible. He clawed at Dez's hands, kicking at the wall, at Dez. Blake didn't stop. Sully's heart pounded out a mad rhythm as his vision clouded and darkened.

A flurry of movement and Eva was on Dez's back, arms wrapped solidly around his neck and head in a sleeper hold. Focused on Eva, Blake released the poker, leaving Sully in a gasping, choking heap on his hands and knees. He forced his eyes up to see Blake slam Eva backward into a wall. She grunted but didn't let go. Blake repeated the move, into the cupboards, the fridge.

By then, Sully had managed a good breath, all he'd allow himself before getting back in there to help Eva. He pushed off the floor, springing toward the struggle and catching the side of Dez's head in a jab. Eva, face registering pain, didn't let go. While she maintained a grip on Dez's head and neck, Sully grabbed at Dez's left arm, twisting out and up. Blake managed a choked gasp of pain as he fell to his knees. Eva rode him down to the floor, not letting up.

She and Sully held on until Dez's body went limp in their grasp. Only then did she allow Dez to slip the rest of the way down and let him out of the chokehold. Her breath heaved as she checked Dez's pulse and dug into her coat pocket.

"You okay?" Sully asked.

Eva removed her hand from her pocket, a set of cuffs dangling from her fingers. "Once you get this bastard out of my husband, I will be."

Sully helped Eva cuff Dez's hands behind his back.

"I don't know if these will hold him," she admitted. "I've seen you when you're amped up on the extra energy from ghosts. Dez is strong enough without having a second spirit in there with him."

Sully shook his head. "When I do it, I can control them so they don't take me over—most of the time, anyway. I've got more energy because I'm using my own and theirs equally. Dez doesn't know how to do that, and probably couldn't even if he wanted to. Blake's the same. He's using Dez's body and strength, not adding to it."

"You sure?"

Sully managed a half-smile. "No. But let's go with my theory anyway, okay? I like it better than the alternative."

Seemingly having decided a handcuffed Dez was still better than his own alternative, Blake—still within Dez when he regained consciousness—stayed where he was. For now, anyway.

Sully knew it, sensing it as much as seeing it. If Blake didn't appear back in front of him in his ghost form, Sully would know he remained where he'd need to stay in order for this plan to work. It was possible his theory about it being harder to climb out than in was on the money, and he supposed he could take some comfort in that.

But very little. No matter which way he thought about it, the situation wasn't great for Dez.

Blake wasn't going to make the walk to the car an easy one. Fully recovered upon regaining consciousness, he tugged futilely at the cuffs as if expecting Dez's body was large and strong enough to snap metal. It wasn't. Blake figured it out by the time he'd taken a few steps out the door, signifying the realization by launching back into full-on fight mode.

He shouldered Eva hard, shoving her away from his right side before turning to Sully.

Sully shoved back, hard, landing Dez on his ass in the snow.

"Enough," Sully snapped. "We need to get something straight, right now. I didn't burn down your house or kill you or your family. Margaret Parsons. Remember her? I'll bet your son would remember."

Dez's upper body shot up from the snow, enough heat emanating from his glare to melt ice. "Fuck you."

Sully took a step forward. "No, fuck *you*. You didn't deserve to die the way you did. I'm not suggesting otherwise. But you should have faced justice for all the things you did. You abused children in your care. Kids who were supposed to be able to trust you to look after them. Kids who had horrible lives and needed someone. You betrayed their trust. You betrayed all of us. Don't you dare play the victim with me."

Blake held Sully's eye for a moment. Only a moment. Then he ducked his head. Ashamed. "You don't understand."

"You can tell us all about it during the trip."

Blake peered back up at him. "Where?"

Sully crouched in front of him, gazed into the face of the brother he loved and searched for him there. Dez was in there somewhere, behind the loathing and suspicion oozing from the expression. For now, though, it was best to focus on Blake. They had Dez back. Everything else, Sully could deal with, one step at a time.

The trick was to get Blake to agree to come quietly. Sully and Eva could control him, but not necessarily without a fight. And every fight came with the possibility of someone getting badly hurt. Though the situation was out of their control, it wouldn't eradicate the pain or guilt if any of them was forced to hurt someone they loved.

Anyway, between what Cecilia had said and the way Blake was watching him now, Sully had drawn a conclusion—one he'd never expected to make.

The violence inside Jim Blake had been created, not born. The drunken monster he'd turned into was a construct of his youth. And who knew what sort of childhood his father had endured?

As Cecilia had said, it wasn't an excuse, but it was an explanation. And Sully had never been ignorant to what he could have become without the Braddocks.

One reply to Blake's question would probably be enough to get Blake to come with them willingly. Maybe it wasn't exactly justice; maybe it would be a greater gift than this man deserved.

But it was Christmas. What better time of year for generosity?

Sully managed a smile he didn't feel. "We're taking you to your family."

11

THE TRIP to the car came with a few challenges of its own, the snow and the darkness tripping them up now and again and Blake tugging against them more than once. But Sully and Eva were far from weak, and while a free Dez was a significant challenge for even the two of them together, a handcuffed Dez was manageable.

Coaxing him into the car was another story, so Sully resorted to a reminder about the purpose for their trip.

Blake wasn't convinced. "How the hell would you know where my family is?"

"I'm a private investigator." Sully nodded toward Eva. "She's a cop. We know how to find them."

It was true, in a manner of speaking—just not necessarily the way Blake was meant to read it. It likely spoke more to longing and desperation to find his loved ones and less to trusting them that he finally let them maneuver him into the back seat.

Sully got in next to him while Eva settled in behind the wheel.

The mid-winter sun had set, casting them in darkness once

the interior light went out with the slam of Eva's door. Dez's eyes, a pale glimmer in the glow from the dashboard, had grown large, as if Blake only now felt the full weight of his predicament.

He turned to Sully. "Where are they?"

"Not far."

"Where?" The question a boom, tearing through the vehicle like a bomb blast.

"Edge Creek," Sully said.

"They're dead. I know they're dead. I saw them."

Sully had hoped to avoid this. As Eva took them away from the Blake farm, Sully sought to better explain, offering a more accurate picture of the situation.

"They are. You're still going to be able to see them."

"How the hell would you know that?"

"I think you know."

Blake snorted. "The psychic bullshit you used to pull? All the whining and crying you did about the people in your room at night? You pulling that on me again?"

Sully sought out Dez's eye in the shadows. "It wasn't bullshit. I see the dead. I always have."

Another snort. "Then you're no less a freak now than you were then."

"Watch your mouth, you son of a bitch," Eva growled.

Dez's head snapped toward her. "What did you say to me?"

Sully sought to deescalate things before they got out of hand. Keep him talking. Just keep him talking, and they'd get to Edge Creek before he knew it.

"We talked to your sister," he said.

Blake's attention returned to him. "Cecilia? She's still alive?"

"Yeah. She lost her eyesight, so she sold her house on Sycamore and move into a place where she can have some care.

Were you looking for her when you went to her house and the farm, or were you hoping to find something else?"

"I want to see her."

"You will, eventually. But not tonight."

"I want to *see* her."

Sully made his voice firmer as Blake had. "Not tonight. She isn't interested in seeing you. She's tried to distance herself from her past. Frankly, I don't blame her."

"Wasn't my fault. None of it was my fault."

"Not when you were a kid. Everything that happened after, that was your fault."

Blake turned away. "You don't understand." His voice had softened.

Sully couldn't help it. He laughed. "I don't understand? I don't understand what? What it's like to suffer abuse? Yeah, you know something, I do. Thanks to you and others like you."

Blake's gaze settled on him again. Though the details of the expression were lost to the darkness, Sully didn't sense the anger he had earlier.

"I know this won't mean much, but it was never my intention to turn out the same as him." It was all he said, no apologies added. Then again, this was Jim Blake. What he'd said was probably as close to an apology as he'd ever offered anyone.

The rage had left him, at least temporarily. He was no longer fighting, no longer pulling at the cuffs, no longer searching for an escape. And Sully was no longer seeing the terrifying man of his memories. This was a man missing his family, regretting his past and longing for something better.

In a police interview situation, this would be a suspect primed to offer up a confession.

Know thy enemy, Sully had once heard. He'd overcome his

fear of ghosts by learning more about the things he saw; he'd use the same tactic now.

"When you went to the farm tonight, you were looking for your father, weren't you?"

Dez's head nodded. "Wasn't there, though. Hasn't been there in years by the looks of it." His head turned back to eye Sully. "He dead too?"

Sully offered a nod of his own. "Yeah. A few years back."

Blake's gaze shifted toward his window, and Sully suspected he saw something other than the glow from the distant city lights. "I figured I'd get a bottle and we'd get drunk together for old time's sake. He wouldn't recognize me like this, wouldn't know this guy. But my old man, he never turned down a drink. Stranger shows up at his house with a twenty-six, he'd be my old man's best friend inside of a minute. I wanted to get a few drinks down him, have a few myself, then spring it on him. Spring it on him good. He's a big guy, but not nearly as big as this one I'm in now. If I'd been like this as a teenager, bet your ass he never woulda touched me. If he had, there wouldn't'a been anything left of him for anyone to find."

"You want payback."

The head snapped toward Sully. "I want justice." The moment of fury faded as quickly as it had come, sending Blake's gaze once again toward the window. "Same thing you probably want from me. I got no idea even now if you're really taking me to my family. You could be turning me in for something, all I know."

"I don't want anything from you," Sully said. "You were unfinished business for me, yeah, but it feels settled now. I was a little kid when I knew you, and I'd built you up in my head to be way bigger than you ever were. I've made some peace now."

Saying it felt true. Felt right. He'd gone to McCoy Falls

harbouring that terrified child inside him. That child was no longer cowering or fearful. As he had with the ghosts, Sully had battled and conquered his fear.

The freedom of it might have made him giddy except for the lingering threat to Dez. Sully could pull Blake out now, could hold him until they reached Edge Creek. But this felt more important, getting the answers he—and their client—needed.

Maybe it was even important Blake be allowed to provide them. Sully didn't care much about him, but if Blake could resolve a few things himself, maybe getting him to cross over would be simpler. In the end, it seemed the best option for everyone.

"If your beef's with your father, why torture the people at the house in McCoy Falls?" Sully asked.

Blake gave a dry, humourless laugh. "I was stuck pacing that empty property for God knows how long, watching life go on around me. I watched block parties I couldn't join, neighbours moving in and out, kids heading off to university, families getting together for holidays and barbecues. I had none of that. No one left. And I couldn't go anywhere or do anything except wonder why my family was gone and I was left behind. You try existing like that and tell me how you'd make out."

Sully pictured it briefly, then stopped. The idea of it—of being trapped on the tiny patch of land where you and your loved ones had died while, all around you, the world went on as if you'd never existed—was nothing short of hell on earth.

Blake wasn't done. "When people built there, I knew the world really had moved on without giving two shits about me. I was still there, but no one knew or cared. It was my property. I hadn't given it up, and they were intruding. I wanted them gone, and I tried to convince them to go. If nothing else, I wanted them to at least acknowledge my existence. The guy—Ciaran—

he's a stubborn asshole. So I started playing with them a little more."

"You were hurting her."

"As I said, I spent years barely existing, no control over anything. Suddenly, there are these people there, intruding on my space. Damn straight, I'm going to enjoy getting some power back. Anyway, I never really hurt her. Not much I can do anymore. Not before now, anyway." He snorted and tugged at the cuffs, the metal clinking behind his back. "Not even now. It wasn't a big jump from goading Ciaran into stuff to stepping into this guy I'm in. I didn't figure getting out would be a problem."

Sully lifted a brow. He'd been right on that count. "Don't worry. When the time comes, I can get you out."

"What, you some sort of exorcist?"

"Not exactly, but I can control spirits."

Blake laughed, the sound mocking rather than amused. "Bull."

Sully focused on Blake's spirit, turning this into both a test for himself and a teaching moment for Blake. He easily felt the edges of Blake's bitter, angry energy—so different from Dez's warmth—and gave it a solid tug. He felt it shift, pull ever so slightly free of Dez. Then he let it go, felt it slam backward, like a boulder tugged free of a hoist and re-ensnared by gravity. Dez's body, held in Blake's grasp, pressed backward toward the door, putting as much space as he could between himself and Sully.

"What the hell are you?"

Sully grinned. "Same as I've always been, only stronger. Lucky for you, it took me a while to really get a handle on my abilities. If I'd had this much power as a kid, you would've liked me a whole lot less."

It felt petty, but he allowed himself to temporarily revel in the other man's fear, in this turning of the tides. Though he could forgive Blake, put his past behind him and find peace in all of it, it didn't mean he couldn't be at least a little immature about it. For someone who'd been forced into adulthood as a young child, a little immaturity now and again should be allowed.

He gave Blake one final smirk, then settled back against the seat, into silence.

12

THE LIGHT WASN'T YET visible when they arrived at the track at the site where the town of Edge Creek had once stood.

The usual series of tire tracks flattening the snow on the approach marked the entrance to the crossing, and Eva had started to pull in when they noticed another vehicle parked there.

Sully hadn't thought of this, and experienced a moment of panic, trying to imagine how they'd be able to lug a handcuffed man to the tracks without anyone questioning them, let alone how he'd be able to complete what amounted to an exorcism and a handover of Blake to the Reaper. Unfortunately, the site—marked as it was by a ghostly, after-dark light—was popular among the ghost-hunting public. The fact recent events had connected deaths with this spot had only increased the fascination for many.

"Damn," Sully said.

Eva pulled on her gloves and removed a small Maglite from the glove compartment. "Don't worry about it. I've got it cased. Wait here with him."

Sully leaned toward her, his thoughts returning to what had

happened the last time they'd been here, what Eva had to do. "Are you sure?"

She turned her head, glancing from Sully to Dez and back again. "Damn sure."

Eva climbed out of the driver's seat, then shut the door and headed toward the tracks, the car's headlights guiding her. Sully watched until she disappeared, walking south along the track to where he assumed the ghost hunters were standing.

Another unfortunate result of the delay was it had given Blake time to think. "Why the hell would my family be here, in the middle of nowhere? What the fuck are you playing at?"

Sully opted for honesty. "They aren't here, not exactly. There's someone here who can help you find them."

It was all Sully had time for. A couple in their late teens came walking at a brisk clip around the corner and climbed into their car, Eva barely stifling a grin behind them.

She dropped back in behind the wheel and reversed out, parking temporarily on the highway's shoulder to allow the couple to similarly back out. The couple's car pulled onto the highway and headed north, toward Kimotan Rapids.

"Didn't take much to convince them to leave," Eva said. "They were already seriously spooked by the time I came around the corner at them. They both screamed like five year olds in an amusement park haunted house."

Sully managed a laugh.

Eva turned to him with a smile. "And just so you know, I'm okay."

The tail lights having disappeared into the distance, Eva pulled back in, taking the spot vacated by the couple. After climbing from the driver's side, she circled the car and opened the rear door, where she could release Dez from the back seat.

Sully stayed put behind him, intending to give him a push out if need be.

He didn't need to. Blake, though far from convinced, was still willing to give this a try. Given what he'd explained about his existence on this side of the afterlife, Sully figured nearly anything else had to be a better alternative. He climbed out with only a little assistance due to the cuffs.

Once all three were out of the car, they made for the track ahead, Dez between them.

"Did you see if the light's out?" Sully asked.

"Wasn't yet," Eva said. "Either they didn't know how to summon it or they were too scared to try. My money's on the latter."

At the rail line, Sully stood between the tracks and clanged the solid handle of Eva's Maglite against one of them three times. Then he straightened, handed it back and waited.

It didn't take long. Ahead, in the distance, a bright light snapped on.

"Better make sure it's not a real train," Eva said. "Check the tracks."

Sully removed a glove, then crouched again to lay his palm against the iron. He could feel no vibration, he knew to play it safe anyway. He'd listen for the sound of an approaching train and step away if he heard anything.

But as the light grew—far more rapidly than a regular train—he knew he'd succeeded in summoning the Reaper.

Eva—and normally Dez—would see the light only. For Sully, as the light reached them, it was something altogether different. He saw a full train, one of those old-fashioned types from around the end of the nineteenth century. It coasted to an unnaturally silent stop, no squealing brakes or hiss of steam to match the light cloud surrounding it. A muted glow emanated from the windows, enough Sully could make out the forms of people inside.

"What the hell?" Blake said. "What is this?"

Sully didn't reply, his focus now on a lean male figure stepping from the nearest carriage. Clothed head to toe in black and wearing a wide-brimmed hat, he had the appearance and bearing of a Wild West lawman—and Sully suspected that was exactly what he had been in life. He moved gracefully and with purpose, one hand hovering near an old-style revolver on his right hip. Sully hadn't noticed it before, and wondered what its use would be against either the living or those who were already dead.

A pair of eerie, coal-black eyes peered into Sully's as the Reaper reached him. Beside Sully, Dez—still in Blake's control—shuddered and took a step back. The Reaper's eyes followed.

"I see you've got a problem here," he said.

Sully had heard him speak before, but was nonetheless as surprised this time as last. His entire life, he'd never heard the dead speak, not unless they were possessing a living person or he was near death himself. There was something different about this spirit. Maybe it was because Sully shared a very similar power, maybe it was because the Reaper was something beyond a typical ghost. Whatever it was, conversation was a good thing.

Even if one's conversational companion was Death personified.

"His name's Jim Blake, and he's possessing my brother," Sully explained.

"And you want me to pull him out for you."

"I can do that myself. I just need you to take him from there."

The Reaper's lips quirked up on one side. "Not my job tonight."

Sully's stomach dropped. All this time, he'd relied on this

moment—on the Reaper—to free Dez. Dread replaced hope. "What?"

The other side of the Reaper's mouth lifted, creating a full smile. "After more than one hundred thirty-five years of riding the rails, I've finally got myself something of a promotion. Means I get to see some new scenery. Got myself what you might call some trainees. Pretty sure you know them."

Two figures appeared out of the mist behind the Reaper, both significantly taller and broader than he was.

The first thing Sully saw clearly was copper hair.

He pressed a hand to his mouth as their faces came into view. His heart jumped, pounding wildly against his ribs as if it wanted to get to them as badly as the rest of him did.

Because the Reaper was right. He did know them.

Flynn and Aiden Braddock.

"How?" Sully asked. It was all he could get out.

"Things are going on in the spirit world, Sullivan," the Reaper said. "Might be a war's brewing. More and more, souls are refusing the light and sticking around down here. Means more reapers will be necessary to find them and haul them in—the bad apples, anyway. Your dad was a lawman with a keen sense of justice. Aiden would have been had he lived long enough. Powers that be gave them the option, and they agreed to help. They'll work under me a while, till they've got a good understanding for the job. For now, the train will be more theirs than mine, freeing me up to hunt. Gotta say, I'm kinda partial to the arrangement."

Though Sully was listening, his eyes had yet to leave Flynn's. Both Flynn and Aiden wore warm smiles, and a peace—one Sully had seen when they'd crossed over a couple of years ago—remained firmly in their expressions.

"Can I talk to them?" Sully asked.

"Of course you can, son," Flynn said.

A breath of cold, winter air caught in Sully's throat. He hadn't heard Flynn's voice in so long, he'd started to worry he'd forgotten it. Hearing it now, it was as if the entire world had disappeared, leaving just them.

"God, I miss you so much," Sully said.

Flynn's smile widened as he shifted his head slightly downward, in Sully's direction. "There's nothing to miss. I've never left you boys or your mother or Dez's girls. I've always been nearby." His eyes moved to Aiden. "We both have."

Aiden beamed. "Now we'll be around a little bit differently." He turned to Dez. The smile disappeared and his eyes narrowed, the greens of his irises suddenly glowing an unnatural black. "Once we get that bastard out of my brother."

Sully held up a hand to stop him. "Leave it to me."

He turned to Dez. His eyes were large, fixed firmly on the two copper-headed spirits, his expression unreadable. Fear dwelled there, clearly Blake's. But something else floated beneath, something truly belonging to Dez.

Joy.

Sully closed the distance to him. "Jim, it's time."

"My family." It was anyone's guess as to who had said the words, Dez or Blake.

The Reaper took a shot at it. "They've crossed over. They've got work to do to make things right, and so will you, but you'll be together."

Blake nodded. "Okay. Okay, good." Then he turned back to Sully. "For what it's worth, I wish I could've been different."

"Me too," Sully said. "For what it's worth, I forgive you."

Then he pulled, dragging Blake's energy from Dez. He focused harder than he ever had before, fighting his natural inclination to suck the energy into himself. This time, once Blake was in the open—leaving Dez collapsed onto his hands and knees in the snow, Eva next to him—Sully worked on pushing out at the same time.

A moment later, he felt release, as if someone had taken a massive weight from him. Aiden had taken charge of Blake and now guided him toward the train.

Blake cast one more glance back, wide, worried eyes locking onto Sully's.

Sully nodded.

Blake nodded back and allowed Aiden to escort him onto the train.

Flynn, when Sully turned, was kneeling next to Dez in the snow, a hand on his back. What Dez felt, if anything, Sully didn't know, but as he got closer, he heard wracking sobs coming from him. Sully closed the rest of the distance and dropped down between Eva and Flynn.

He placed a hand against Dez's head and gently tried to coax it upward. "Dez? Are you okay? Talk to me, man."

"He's okay," Eva said. Her smile backed up her claim. "I mean, he's *really* okay. Believe me, this is him super happy. He said he saw his dad and brother."

Flynn peered at Sully. "He saw us because Blake saw us. I doubt he can anymore. Tell him we're still here."

The Reaper's voice sounded behind them. "Flynn? One day soon, you'll be able to tell him yourself."

Sully jumped as the Reaper's hand settled on his shoulder—a touch he felt physically.

"Reapers move between worlds," the spirit explained. "Because of that, we can become corporeal when we need to."

Though the hand remained, the feel of it faded. Corporeal to spirit, just like that.

"Flynn?" he said. "We need to go. You can return soon."

Flynn nodded and stood, giving Sully a smile. “Tell Dez and Eva and your mom and Kayleigh how much we love them. And I love you too, kiddo. Thanks for taking care of your brother.”

“I love you too,” Sully said. “As for taking care of Dez, it’s what I do best.”

Flynn beamed. “Damn straight.”

Then he turned and followed the Reaper back to the train.

13

THE TRAIN FADED and the light with it. Sully returned to Dez and Eva.

They were back on their feet, Dez's tear-filled eyes fixed to the spot where, moments ago, their dad had stood. Eva's arms were wrapped around his barrel of a chest, and he had one long arm around her, holding her to him. His other now snagged Sully and hauled him in too.

They stood there for a solid minute or two, a group hug that restored some needed warmth. A light snow began to fall, the night cold biting into exposed flesh. Sully's tears froze on his cheeks. It didn't matter. All that mattered was this, standing here with two of the people he loved more than anything in this world, sharing the knowledge Flynn and Aiden were more fully back in their world—in a manner of speaking, anyway.

Dez at last gave a shuddering sigh, releasing Sully and Eva before scrubbing at his own face.

"God, I'm so cold," came a partially muffled statement from behind his hands.

Sully patted him on the back. "Let's get you two back home to Kayleigh."

They fell into a temporary silence as they returned to the car, Sully taking the back seat so Dez could have the front passenger seat, nearer the heat vents. Eva cranked them on full before pulling back onto the highway.

She placed a hand on Dez's leg. "Are you hurt? Do you need me to take you to a hospital?"

He shook his head. "Not physically. Everything else, though … God, I'm sorry. I'm so sorry. I was there. I saw it all happening. I'm so sorry, Evie."

"Don't." Her voice was firm, the tone allowing no argument. "It wasn't your fault. It wasn't you."

"But I was *there*." He turned far enough to allow him to reach into the back seat and grasp Sully's knee. "I thought I killed you. I really did. Back at the house in McCoy Falls. I thought—" Tears again filled Dez's eyes, and he turned away to swipe at them with his free hand.

Sully pried Dez's fingers from his leg and gave them a squeeze. "Like Eva said, not your fault. Believe me, no one understands possession as well as I do. I nearly took you out once the same way, remember? Consider this the universe evening the score."

He'd said the last part tongue in cheek, hoping for a laugh, but it was clear from Dez's glare he wasn't yet in the laughing mood. "It wasn't a score I ever wanted to even."

"I know. I'm sorry. I was kidding."

"Well, don't. This whole day has been a nightmare." He paused. "Or it was until a few minutes ago. That was real, right? What I saw? It wasn't some trick of my mind?"

Sully gave Dez's hand one last squeeze and released it. "It

was real. Dad and Aiden have found themselves a new occupation."

This time, Dez did laugh. "Leave it to Dad to find a way to stay a cop, even in the afterlife." He'd been facing front again, but now turned back to Sully. "You mentioned a couple of years ago Aiden had grown up. I couldn't picture it. God, it was amazing, seeing him like that."

Dez's eyes filled again, and he pinched at the corners of his eyes to stem this latest flow. "Bloody hell, I'm a wreck."

Eva patted his leg. "In a good way."

Dez cast another glance over his shoulder. "How dangerous is it, do you think, what they're doing? I mean, I know they're already dead and everything, but can ghosts hurt other ghosts? Is there a chance something bad could happen to them?"

"I don't know, Dez," Sully said. "I don't have any answers. All I can say for sure is the Reaper said he's been doing it for over a hundred thirty years, and he seems perfectly fine to me. And Dad wouldn't let Aiden get into anything he thought would put him at risk."

Eva chuckled. "Hey, given what you told me about him, I don't think a guy his size is going to be easily ordered around."

Dez grinned. "I'm still taller."

"Jury's out," Eva said. "If I ever get to see him, I'm insisting on a back-to-back measurement."

Sully hated to break up a happy moment, but he had an apology of his own to make. "Hey, D? I'm sorry about insisting we go to McCoy Falls. I had a bad feeling about going back there, and I should have paid attention."

Dez met his eye. "Did you make some peace with what happened to you there as a kid?"

"Yeah, I did, but—"

"No buts. If you've laid that part of your life to rest, it was worth it. Granted, there are a lot of things I wish hadn't happened, but the outcome turned out okay, right? You've come to terms with what happened to you and we got to see Dad and Aiden. And …" He trailed off, eyes widening as if some new horror had occurred to him. "Oh God. I shoplifted. I ran out of a liquor store with a bottle of booze. And I got the SUV stuck. Eva and Kayleigh's presents are in there. Oh crap, they *better* still be in there."

"Relax," Sully said. "The SUV was fine. We'll get a tow tomorrow. And I smoothed everything over already with the liquor store and paid for the bottle. You're good."

Dez released his breath in a whoosh. "The presents though."

Eva made a show of bouncing around in her seat. "What did you get me?"

"You'd better get the chance to find out."

Sully reached forward to pat Dez on the shoulder. "Don't worry. Once you guys get home, I'll take a cab back to my place and drive out to McCoy Falls. I should try to meet up with our client to fill her in. If you give me your keys, I'll get everything out of your SUV on the way."

"You're not taking a cab," Eva said. "I'll drop you off on the way through."

It said something about the frayed state of Dez's nerves and emotions that he didn't argue he should also be present to meet with Lisa. Sully wouldn't have allowed it, anyway. Dez needed to be with Eva and Kayleigh. That and a hot meal and a warm bath, in whichever order Eva deemed best. Dez would be in good hands.

"Come to our place once you're done in McCoy Falls," Dez said.

"It'll be late."

"I don't care. I mean it. I'm going to call Mom too. I want my family together."

Sully gave Dez's shoulder a squeeze. "Sounds good to me."

Sully saw Dez and Eva off in the parking lot behind his building, then called Lisa's cellphone as he drove out of town in his own SUV.

"Hey," he said. "Great news. It's over. The man who was bothering you is gone. We got him crossed over."

"So he won't be back?"

"His family was already over there. He's gone to be with them. He won't bug you again."

A sob erupted from the other side of the line. "Oh my God, you have no idea. Oh my God, thank you so, so much! This is the best Christmas present ever!"

Sully laughed. "I'm heading in your direction to check on a vehicle we left on a back road. Is there anything you need me there for? I'm happy to come and sit down and take you through everything."

"No, it's okay. Some things I think I'd rather not know. Anyway, I'd still be happier if Ciaran didn't find out about me calling you. I mean, I'll have to explain it eventually, given the money and all, but that's a problem for later. It's weird though. He came home and he's been lovely, like he was before we moved in here. The whole place feels different, lighter somehow. And so does Ciaran."

Sully knew exactly what she meant. "The ghost who was haunting you guys told me he was influencing Ciaran. I have no doubt you'll find your relationship will go back to what it used to be."

Lisa gave a little laugh, one choked by emotion. "I wish I could give you a big hug. You have no idea. I'll check in with Mr. Fields tomorrow for whatever else I might owe. I'll pay anything, seriously."

"No worries. Happy to help. Really. It turned out okay for me too, actually." He smiled into the phone. "I guess we all laid some ghosts to rest."

The SUV was still where it had been, stuck in the snow near the grid. It occurred to Sully only now, as he retrieved the bags containing the gifts for Eva and Kayleigh, that he had no idea why Blake had driven this way in the first place.

He glanced up at the approach of headlights, his brows lifting as what appeared to be a half-ton truck parked next to his SUV, left behind on the main grid.

Sully headed back the short distance and found a man emerging from the pickup truck.

"Having trouble?" the man asked. The suspicion was there. And the way the truck door remained open, the man within easy reach to the seat, Sully figured he had a gun available.

Sully planted on his friendliest smile. "I was out here earlier, looking for a buddy of mine. We found his vehicle stuck and followed his footprints to a nearby farm."

"What did he look like?" the man asked. Testing him.

"Really tall, red hair."

The man visibly relaxed and shut the door to his half-ton, sealing both the warmth and any potential weapons inside. Test passed.

The man offered his hand. "I'm Keith. I think my wife mentioned to you, I drove your buddy to some farm land south of KR. I'm sorry to say, he seemed a little off to me." Keith gave a sheepish smile. "I kinda left him there. I didn't feel right about something."

"It's okay. He was having some problems today. But we found him, and he's doing a lot better. I'm sorry if he gave you any grief. He's not normally like that."

The explanation seemed good enough for Keith, given he moved to lean on Sully's hood to gaze and nod toward Dez's SUV, illuminated in Sully's headlights. "I came to check and see how bad the vehicle's stuck. Figured I might be able to use my frontend loader to tow it out of there tomorrow, if you want."

Sully beamed. "That would be awesome, thanks."

Keith returned the grin. "No worries. Let me know when you want to come out and I'll meet you."

"It's Christmas Eve tomorrow," Sully said. "How about we meet you earlier in the day? That way, hopefully we won't be interfering in your day as much."

Keith agreed and they set a time for eight in the morning. Dez would hate the idea of dragging himself up so early to come out here, but he'd get over it.

They were about to head their separate ways for the night when it occurred to Sully Keith might have an answer to his recent question.

"The road where my buddy got stuck, where does it lead?" he asked. "Is there anything down there?"

"Used to be a farm," Keith said. "Guy named Jim Blake lived there with his wife and son. They moved into town when the kid was ready to start school. Someone bought the farmhouse and moved it somewhere else." Keith frowned. "Can't say I was sorry to see the back of him. The guy was a real asshole. Guess I shouldn't speak ill of the dead, though."

14

Sully and Eva headed out early the next morning, Eva having snuck out before Dez woke up.

"He's exhausted," she said while Sully drove them out of the city to meet with Keith and his frontend loader. "Yesterday took a lot out of him." She hugged her arms across her middle. "It took a lot out of all of us."

Sully cast her a glance. "You doing okay?"

"Better, but I'm already tired of dealing with Dez's guilt. He remembers tossing me around, and I don't think he's ever going to forget it."

"Take advantage. Get him to take you to Paris or something."

Eva grinned at his joke. "Right. Can you see Dez trailing behind me through the Louvre and Montmartre? It would be a nightmare—and not just for him. For me, too, and everyone around us."

Sully conceded her point with a laugh. "Point taken. But seriously, how are you doing?"

Though she didn't meet his eye, he sensed her understanding in the shift of her body in the seat. "You mean about what I told you yesterday? I'm okay. I really am. It always feels a little awkward to talk about, but I don't mind you knowing. I'll always be dealing with it in one way or another. It'll never fully go away, but I've got a little box where I can put it so it doesn't affect every other aspect of my life. Once in a while, the box gets opened. I know I can put it back again when it does."

Her eyes met his for the moment he could spare from the road. "How about you?" she asked. "How are you?"

He'd been trying to put it into words inside his own brain, to make sense of everything that had happened. He wasn't sure he had the right words even now. He gave it a shot anyway. "I feel guilty saying this, because I hate what Dez went through and what we went through as a result. But being able to have a real conversation with Blake and to learn why he became what he did, it's helped me. A lot. Evil becomes less evil when you can explain it in human terms. What he and his family put their foster kids through—what they put each other through, for that matter—was horrible. But now I can see the path that led him there. His actions turned him into a monster inside my head. Suddenly, he's become human. My fear is gone as a result. I made my peace with him, and I guess I made some peace with myself too."

Eva's hand grasped his for a moment, gripping the backs of his fingers on the steering wheel. "You'll have bad moments sometimes, like when you find yourself dealing with kids who are suffering abuse. But our pasts don't need to define who we are the rest of the time."

He smiled. "You're right, except it does kind of define me. I understand fear and pain and helplessness because of the Blakes. I understand the need for justice and doing what's right. It's knowledge I carry with me every time I deal with a ghost who's lost their life to homicide. Maybe that common connection is part of why I see them, why I can help them. Why it's important to me to help them." He caught her eye. "And the Blakes are one of the reasons I will always be grateful for my family. There's not a lot of good in a past like mine, but it helps me to appreciate the present. And that, at least, isn't a bad thing."

Eva gave his hand another squeeze.

"No," she said. "It isn't."

It happened while they were sitting around the television that night in Dez and Eva's basement, the black and white version of *Scrooge* in the Blu-ray player.

The doorbell rang, causing Dez to wake abruptly on the floor where he was lying between Eva and Pax. Pax let out a bark and charged for the stairs.

"I'll get it," Sully volunteered. "I'll get Pax while I'm at it."

"Could you bring me a glass of water on your way down, sweetie?" his mom asked.

"Water?" Dez chided. "It's Christmas Eve, Mom. Stop being so healthy and have something fun."

Sully jogged up the stairs, leaving his family to debate the merits of drink choices.

They'd had their usual group of friends over for an early Christmas dinner, saving tomorrow for family. Sully had just returned from driving his neighbour, Emily Crichton, home, allowing Mara Braddock to start her annual Christmas tradition of sitting down with the family to watch the 1951 version of the Dickens classic.

Sully wondered if he'd parked haphazardly upon his return, and a neighbour was here to complain. The snowbanks along the sidewalk made proper parking difficult.

He wasn't prepared for who he found standing on the porch.

"Jack gave us the night off," Flynn said. "We wanted to spend it with you guys."

Tears clouded Sully's vision as Flynn and Aiden passed by him, into the front entry. Aiden pushed the door shut while Pax licked at Flynn's hand.

"Wait a minute," Sully said. "You're real?"

Flynn laughed. "We've always been real, son."

"No, I meant, you're not just ghosts?"

The answer came as Flynn pulled him into a hug, a very real hug. A sob escaped Sully's throat as he grabbed his dad back, feeling him there, solid and strong and full of life. A different kind of life, but life all the same.

"We could have kind of materialized downstairs, but we figured Mom and Dez would crap themselves," Aiden said.

Sully went from crying to laughing, then finally pulled away from Flynn to share a hug with Aiden. "You got that right. Give me a few seconds to fill them in. Can you stay like this? Solid, I mean, so they can see you?"

"For a while," Flynn said. "It takes a surprising amount of energy to stay this way, and we need to be sharp when we go back. Just like policing, Christmas is a busy time of year for this kind of work, unfortunately."

Sully nodded. Any sadness he felt at the truth of Flynn's statement disappeared as he thought of the expressions on his family's faces a minute from now. He and Dez had told their mom and Kayleigh about having seen Flynn and Aiden, and while Mara was thrilled for them, Sully had seen the sadness there too, the realization she hadn't been—and might never be—able to see her husband and son again.

"Maybe you should let me kind of prepare them," Sully said. "Aiden's right. Mom's going to freak out."

Flynn smiled. “I hear ya.”

Sully patted Flynn on the chest, allowing himself a moment to linger there, revelling in the solid feel of flesh and bone beneath his fingers. Then he returned to the basement where Mara had paused the movie to wait for him.

“Who was it?” Eva asked.

“You didn’t bring my water,” Mara observed.

Sully grinned. “Hey, guys, don’t freak out, but there’s someone here you’re going to want to see.”

Behind him, Flynn emerged from the stairs. Any fear Sully had harboured that maybe Flynn and Aiden wouldn’t be visible to the others disappeared as Mara’s hands shot to her mouth. She sobbed when Aiden pushed in next to Flynn.

Dimples popped on Aiden’s freckled cheeks as he beamed at her. “Hey, Mom.”

Mara fired off the couch and rushed toward them, Dez immediately behind. Sully gave them a moment, watching with happy tears as the Braddocks embraced each other—all four of them for the first time since Aiden’s murder at age five.

Sully joined Eva and a mystified-looking Kayleigh. “That’s Uncle Aiden? I thought he was little. He’s huge like Dad.”

“Is he ever,” Eva said. “I think spirits get a chance to grow up too, hon.” She leaned in closer to Sully. “Don’t tell Dez, but I think he was right. He is still bigger.”

Sully chuckled as Kayleigh rushed over and wedged herself into the group hug, arms around what she could reach of her grandfather’s middle. He broke up the hug to gather her into his arms properly, lifting her from the floor the way he used to. Then he set her down and released her with one arm so he could draw Eva in as well.

Dez stood next to Aiden, arm slung around his shoulders

while he waited for Flynn to finish. "Hey, Aidy, there are a couple people I want you to meet."

"Dez, dude, I've been with you your whole life. I know Eva and Kayleigh pretty damn well already."

Even so, Aiden knelt to introduce himself properly to Kayleigh. "Hey, kiddo. You don't know me, but I'm your uncle Aiden."

Kayleigh giggled and threw her arms around his neck. "Of course I know you. Dad talks about you all the time."

Mara, arms wrapped around Flynn's middle, wore an expression of joy, the likes of which Sully had never seen gracing her face. Always pretty, now it seemed as if ten years and a ton of emotional weight had dropped from her.

"How long can you stay?" she asked Flynn.

"The boys told you what we're doing now?"

"We did," Sully said. "We knew they'd want to know."

Flynn nodded. "We can't stay long, though we'll be able to come by sometimes for a visit. I'll be honest. Part of why we decided to take the gig was this—the chance to be able to hug you all again, and so you could see Aiden for yourselves and know we're both fine."

"Is it dangerous, what you're doing?" Mara asked.

"Nothing we can't handle. Anyway, Jack's good at what he does, and he's been doing it a long time."

"Who's Jack?" Mara asked.

"He's the fellow in charge of the train," Flynn said. "Jack Winter. Apparently, he earned himself a nickname during his old lawman days—Tracker Jack. He did what Sully does now—using ghosts to bring bad guys to justice. He's just got a different way of tracking them as a spirit." Flynn smiled. "I guess Aidy and I do too."

He pulled away far enough he could face Mara. "Listen,

Mare, this whole Reaper thing is kind of new to me, so I don't know how it all works. But I will always do my best to come and see you whenever I can. And who knows, maybe sometimes, Death really will be able to take a holiday."

Sully rolled his eyes and Dez and Aiden gave a mutual groan.

"Come on," Flynn said through a laugh. "It was funny."

Flynn and Aiden stayed for the movie, although Sully guessed no one watched it, everyone's eyes straying to each other and conversation passing as if to assure themselves this was really happening. At the end of it, they stood and gave each other long parting hugs.

"Want us to leave through the door?" Aiden asked. "Or would you rather see us book it the cool way?"

For Kayleigh, at least, the answer was obvious. "Do it the cool way!"

Aiden gave a big toothy grin. He waved, then promptly disappeared, leaving his grin hanging there, bodiless for a full five seconds before it too was gone.

Flynn rolled his eyes. "That kid. He's such a dork. Listen, we'll see you all again soon. Sleep well and merry Christmas."

Then he blinked out too.

Dez stepped to Sully's side. "Do you still see them?"

Sully shook his head. "No, they're gone. They must have returned to the train."

Eva turned to Kayleigh. "Okay, kid, time for bed."

Kayleigh groaned but followed Eva anyway, Pax trotting along beside.

"He always sleeps on Kayleigh's bed," Dez said. "We finally

decided we'd have to buy her a bigger one since Pax takes up so much damn room."

Mara gave Dez and Sully one more hug, then made her way upstairs to the spare room. Sully didn't think the smile once left her face.

Dez pulled open a hutch along the wall and dug out a quilt for Sully to use on the downstairs couch. He didn't say anything as he spread it out.

"You okay?" Sully asked.

Dez nodded and smiled. "Yeah. I am. I was feeling pretty awful about stuff, but seeing Dad and Aiden, it made things better."

"You don't have anything to feel awful about. I need you to understand. That world isn't one most people are meant to interact with, not the way you were forced to. Nothing was your fault."

Dez dropped his head, gave it a shake, then lifted it again. A humourless smile twisted his lips. "Yeah, but I saw it all, Sull. And I couldn't do a damn thing. Yeah, you had it happen to you before, but the difference was you stopped it. I tried. I couldn't. It was like being chained down in the back seat of my own car with some maniac behind the wheel."

"I know, I get it. But Dez, we're different, you and me. I've always been a part of that world, and I've got abilities you don't. You can't compare the way the two of us dealt with it. You not being able to stop Blake, it's not about weakness or failure. Sometimes bad things happen to us, and no matter what we do, we can't change it. Being strong isn't always about stopping the bad things. It's about what we do after. You were my strength at times in my life when I didn't have any of my own. Hell, you still are. I know you, and you're strong enough to get through this. But let me help, okay? Blake was my problem, and he made himself yours. I want to help fix things."

"Wrong," Dez said. "If Blake was your problem, then he was *our* problem. We're brothers, Sull. Means your problems are mine too." He smiled, a real one this time. "And I know. It works the other way around as well."

He pulled Sully into a hug. "I promise I'll be fine. I'm not happy about how things went yesterday, and I might always carry a little guilt, but I'll be fine. Just like I know you will be. Merry Christmas, Sull."

Sully gripped Dez back, hard, relief flooding him at the honesty in Dez's words. "Merry Christmas, Dez."

COMING IN APRIL 2021

DEAD MAN'S LAKE

Chapter 1

Adam Charles steered over the ice, one hand balancing a small container of maggots on the centre console as the half-ton bounced across heaves and dips.

His usual fishing hole lay up ahead, the tiny ice fishing shack marking the spot. It was mid-morning, and the sun was out, reflecting off the snow in a way that had him reaching for his sunglasses. He usually liked an earlier start, preferring to be out here with his line in the water before sun-up. But he had his son this weekend, and nine-year-old boys weren't as easily convinced about the benefits of early rising.

Adam glanced toward his passenger. If Tristan sensed his father's eyes on him, he didn't let on. He was beaming, eyes fixed expectantly on the shack ahead.

"How's fishing been?" the boy asked at last.

Adam smiled. "Been good. Mostly pike biting, but I got a trout last weekend. Nice one too. Thought we could fry it up tonight, unless you catch us something today."

Tristan nodded, rapidly enough to reveal his enthusiasm for the plan. Most kids of Adam's acquaintance didn't mind casting a line in a few times, but they soon tired of hanging out on a frozen lake with limited internet service and nothing to listen to but stories and a battery-powered radio perpetually tuned to an oldies station. Not Tristan, though. He happily stayed out here all day, would stay longer if it wasn't for Adam's insistence they needed to go make themselves a proper meal at home. What was more, Tristan actually enjoying eating the fish he caught, didn't even mind the gutting and cleaning process.

Adam had helped create a kid who was like a smaller, younger version of himself. While that likely presented some frustration to the boy's mother, Adam's ex, it suited him just fine. He never felt so proud as when other fishermen, entering the fishing shack to inquire after their day's catch, remarked on the fact Adam had a son who actually wanted to be out here with him.

"It would take an act of God to get my kid to come fishing," one man said virtually every time he stopped by.

"Not my Tristan," Adam would say. "He's a better fisherman than I am."

At which, Tristan would grin and Adam would match it with his own nearly identical expression.

A handful of fishing shacks were out here besides their own, scattered here and there around this part of the large lake. One guy Adam didn't know had annoyingly plunked his structure down very near to Adam's since the last time he'd come. He saw no sign of anyone there at the moment, no vehicles present next to it, and Adam briefly entertained a fantasy involving him nosing his truck up next to the small building and pushing it to the middle of the lake.

Tristan, it seemed, was no happier about their new neighbour. "Why is that guy so close?"

Adam corralled his own annoyance at the situation, locking it away before answering. He was, after all, the adult. "Plenty of room for all of us. Anyway," he added with a wink at his son, "He's not here yet. Let's get ourselves set up fast so we can catch all the fish before he comes."

Tristan laughed. "Yeah!"

Twenty minutes later, and they were parked and shut inside the shack, gradually warming thanks to the propane-powered space heater. Adam had drilled the fishing hole back open and the two of them were sitting on either side of it, lines in the water, in companionable silence. Adam would ask later how Tristan was doing in school, how his mom was, how he was getting along with his stepdad and step-siblings, whether he still liked the same girl in his class. But for now, they would just sit here quietly, happy to be together.

Adam checked his watch. Shortly after ten in the morning. A good, long day lay ahead of them, the stretch of hours a blessing.

Two hours and Adam was removing his line to dig into the cooler he'd brought with their lunches. He'd made sandwiches and had poured hot chicken noodle soup into a pair of thermoses for them.

He started to hand Tristan his, but the boy shook his head. "Ten more minutes," he said. "I've got a feeling."

Adam uttered a closed-mouthed chuckle, the sound rumbling

up from his chest. "Don't wait too long. Soup's still warm, but it won't stay that way."

Tristan nodded, then resumed fishing.

Adam had polished off his lunch before Tristan even removed his line from the water.

"Still have a feeling?" Adam ribbed his son.

"Five more minutes," Tristan replied.

Adam stood. "Okay. I've got to go visit the little boy's tree. When I get back, you'd better eat something."

Tristan nodded but didn't otherwise reply, and Adam left the shack to begin the short walk to shore and the clustering of spindly bushes and trees—drowned during the floods a few years back—that served as a bathroom for him and Tristan. He walked in, following his old trail in the snow through bunches of willow, branches tugging at his coat and jeans as he pushed through. Reaching his usual spot, he unzipped and relieved himself, then kicked snow over the expended urine before turning to go back.

He ducked again and shouldered his way through the willow. Free of the trees with the lake's ice beneath him, he straightened and sought out the shack.

A man stood next to it, facing him.

Adam jumped, not so much because of the unexpected and sudden appearance, but because of something in the man's presence.

He stood rigidly upright but his arms hung lifelessly at his sides. From here, it seemed as if small pieces of his face were gone, like something had been nibbling at his flesh. But it was the ice that really struck Adam—or rather, the fact it covered the man from head to toe. It clung to his jeans and his red and black checked jacket, coated his brows and beard and turned his hair into an array of white spikes.

As Adam took a few reluctant steps forward, he found more to concern him. The man's mouth was drawn back in a horrifying grimace, lips pulled taut and teeth clenched together between them. And the eyes, which Adam would have described at a distance as a pale blue, were actually covered over by a milky film—the sort of film he'd seen on dead bodies in scary movies or cop shows.

Adam was looking at a dead man.

He bit back a scream, knowing his son was within hearing distance. If it wasn't for the fact Tristan was here, Adam would sprint for his truck, jam the keys into the ignition and get the hell out of here.

That wasn't an option.

It *really* wasn't an option. His son Tristan was in the shack right next to the man, and his safety came before anything else.

Adam ran forward, toward the cabin, struggling to keep from looking at the dead man and failing miserably. Every second that passed with that ghastly image in his peripheral vision etched the memory into his brain.

Adam knew exactly what he would see when he closed his eyes tonight.

Passing within just feet of the spectre, he opened and pushed through the door. He wasn't a religious man, but as he slammed it shut behind him, he caught himself praying to God the dead man would stay outside.

"Dad?" Tristan asked. "I caught something … kind of weird."

Adam halted his son with a raised hand. "Just a second, Tris." He edged forward, toward the wall on the right. A small window allowed light in and would provide Adam with a glimpse in the direction where he'd seen the man. He moved silently, listening. The snow settled over the ice would make it impossible for anyone to walk silently. If the man had moved, Adam would have heard it.

Yet, when he peered out the window, there was nothing to see. The man, who moments ago had appeared an eerily solid mass, was gone.

"Dad?"

Adam held a finger to his lips. "Ssh."

"What's wrong?" Tristan whispered.

Adam didn't answer, not yet. He didn't want to scare the boy, yet he wasn't sure how he was going to avoid it. They couldn't stay here, not now. Adam wouldn't have a moment's peace now, sitting here, wondering.

For now, though, he had to know. If the man outside was looking to harm them—to harm Tristan—Adam needed to act.

He searched the dim interior, ignoring the questioning look on Tristan's face as he scanned their belongings for something to use as a weapon. His eyes settled on the small makeshift club he used to kill the fish they caught, and he snatched it up before turning back to the door.

"Dad?" Tristan's voice contained a ring of fear. Adam wanted to say something to alleviate his son's worry but could think of nothing that wouldn't be a boldfaced lie.

"Stay here," Adam said. He took a deep breath, then a second, releasing each in a huff through his nose. Then, his nerves as steady as they'd ever be under the current circumstances, he threw open the door and burst outside.

The man was gone. He wasn't where he'd been standing and he wasn't anywhere else, either. The lake, as far as the eye could see, was bare, save the distant fishing shacks. The one so near his was still empty as well, the padlock visible even from here.

Most startlingly, as Adam scanned the spot where the man

had stood, he saw no trace of footprints, nor any leading from the location.

Nothing to tell him what he'd seen had been anything more than a particularly vivid hallucination.

Adam lowered the bat, letting it dangle at his side as if it weighed half a ton.

"What the …" He let the muttered statement trail off, turning his mind over what he'd seen.

Or hadn't seen. He had been having trouble sleeping lately, after all. It was possible his mind had been playing tricks. Sure, the man had looked real enough, but Adam had heard about people having similar experiences before, ones that turned out to be nothing more than a trick of the mind.

No man. No footprints. Nothing to indicate he'd ever been here.

Adam drew in a long breath, held it as he urged his heart rate to slow. That's all this was, he told himself. Just a trick of the mind. Nothing more.

"Get a grip on yourself," he muttered.

As if to further convince himself, he gave his head a shake and uttered a humourless chuckle. Then he returned to the shack.

Tristan's eyes were wide as the door opened, and Adam sought to relieve his son's anxiety.

"It's all right," he said. "I thought I saw something, that's all."

"What did you see?"

Adam shook his head. "Nothing much. Don't worry about it."

He'd never been much of a fibber, had promised his kid once that he would never lie to him. It felt wrong now, being anything less than honest. But he told himself it would do no good. Better

Tristan not know. No sense scaring him when there was nothing there to fear.

He sought instead to distract the boy, to turn his mind from questions Adam didn't know how to answer. "What were you trying to tell me?"

"I said I caught something weird. Not like a boot or anything. Something else."

Okay, this Adam could cope with. He'd check out Tristan's unusual catch, they'd have a laugh about it and they'd go back to fishing. It would be like nothing had happened.

"All right," he said. "Let's see what you found."

Tristan lifted his ice-fishing pole from where it lay next to the hole. Adam took it from him, eyes travelling the length of the line to what had caught on the hook.

His heart slammed against his ribcage, the pole slipping from his fingers. Adam took a step back, away from the pole and hook as his wide-eyed focus held firm.

There was no question in his mind what he was looking at. Black and red checks stood out in a stream of sunlight coming through the window.

It was a piece of the dead man's jacket.

Chapter 2

Dez Braddock looked up from the stove at the sound of his wife's footsteps entering the kitchen of their Kimotan Rapids house. Eva had still been asleep when he got up, and he'd tried not to wake her while he stepped into their bathroom for a shower. It had been a late night for her, aiding the KRPD's gang unit with an after-hours search warrant.

Dez smiled a greeting. "How'd it go last night?"

"Pretty well," she said. "We took five mid-level players off the streets and a large pile of meth, firearms and ammo. We almost had a higher-up, but he managed to bail right before we got there. Not to worry. One of his guys ratted him out. The G-unit has enough to bust him on some pretty serious charges. Just need to find him now. What about you? How was your day yesterday?"

Dez turned back to his fried eggs, flipping them as he replied. "Nothing exciting."

It was true. Working for renowned retired-cop-turned-PI Lachlan Fields came with some pretty decent jobs, but there were plenty of duds too. Yesterday had involved Dez and his brother, Sullivan Gray, spelling each other as they conducted surveillance on a man suspected to be faking an injury to draw workers' compensation. They'd grabbed a few photos, suggestive but not conclusive. Dez guessed he knew what Lachlan would have them doing later today.

Eva knew Dez well, and he smiled as her arms slid around his waist. "You still miss being a cop, don't you?"

"Days like yesterday, you bet I do." He placed the cooked eggs onto a plate, then returned the pan to the stove before turning to meet Eva's embrace. He leaned down to kiss her, taking some solace in the softness of her lips and the aftertaste of toothpaste.

"God, you guys," came a voice from the other side of the room. "You're too old for that."

Dez glanced up and chuckled as Kayleigh, their nine-year-old daughter, walked in, just out of bed and in search of something to drink. Dez pulled a cup from the cupboard as Kayleigh removed a carton of orange juice from the fridge.

"We are not too old," Dez said.

Kayleigh rolled her eyes, but a smile plucked at her lips. "Whatever, Dad." She filled her cup, then replaced the carton in the fridge before carrying her juice upstairs, presumably to get ready for school.

Eva returned her attention to Dez. "Are you really that bored working for Lachlan?"

"I don't mind it most of the time," Dez said. "But things have been slow lately. Besides, Lachlan always gives Sully and me the jobs he doesn't want."

"He's the boss. That's his prerogative."

"I know, but still."

Eva patted him on the chest. "I'm sure it'll pick up soon. It always does."

"I hope so."

The doorbell rang just as the sound of the water running suggested Kayleigh was in the shower.

Dez glared at the front door as their dog, Pax, came bounding down the stairs, barking. "That kid always gets here a solid half-hour before Kayleigh's ready to leave."

Eva's smile was a knowing one. "He wants to make sure she doesn't leave for school without him. Face it, Dez, he's got a crush. Our girl's a looker."

"That's what I'm afraid of."

Eva yelled to Pax to quiet before patting Dez on the chest. "They're nine. Relax."

"They won't be nine forever."

Eva gave Dez a warning look before heading for the stairs to go get dressed. "Be nice."

"I'm always nice."

Dez waited until his PJ-clad wife was out of sight before answering the front door. "Hi, Tristan."

The kid took part in the usual brief, playful wrestling match with Pax. Then his eyes travelled up Dez's body, neck craned back in an attempt to meet his eye. It was a difficult task even for many adults, Dez's six-and-a-half feet making him stand out in a crowd. Added to his solid frame of muscle, he thought he made for a fairly imposing man—of particular benefit now that his little girl was the object of at least one crush.

Tristan, it seemed, hadn't gotten the memo. "Hi, Mr. Braddock. Can I come in?"

Tristan always asked. As much as Dez felt called upon to play protective dad, this kid had a way of disarming him and drawing a smile from him.

"Yeah," Dez said. "Come on in."

Tristan took off his shoes and trailed Dez into the kitchen. "You having breakfast?"

"Yep," Dez said. Another thing that rarely failed. Tristan almost always made it here in time for breakfast. "You eat yet?"

"Not really. I wasn't exactly hungry yet."

Dez nodded slowly as he eyed the kid. *Sure, you weren't hungry*, he thought. *You just knew the offerings would be better over here.*

Tristan hefted himself onto one of the barstools at the kitchen island and watched as Dez popped the bacon he'd already fried into the microwave to warm up. There was no point waiting on Kayleigh; she'd become a finicky eater and rarely ate more than a bowl of cereal in the mornings. The bacon and eggs were for Dez and Eva—and, apparently, Tristan.

Tristan who tended to stare shyly at Dez more than talk.

"How was your weekend?" Dez asked, more to avoid the silence than because he expected an interesting answer.

"It was kind of weird."

Dez spared the boy a glance over his shoulder in between feeding slices of bread into the toaster. "Weird, how?"

"Dad and I went fishing."

"You guys go fishing a lot, don't you?"

"Yeah, but it was weird this time."

Dez resisted the eye-roll and the exact repeat of his previous question. "In what way?"

"I caught something, but it wasn't a fish. It was a piece of cloth, but it freaked Dad out really bad. He didn't want to stay after. I could tell."

"Because of the piece of cloth?"

"Because of the ghost."

That had Dez's attention. He turned fully toward Tristan to ask the obvious next question. "What ghost?"

"The one at Dead Man's Lake. Everyone's heard of him."

"Dead Man's Lake? That's where you were fishing?"

"Yeah. They stock it with trout as well as pike. I like trout better. You can catch pike *anywhere*." Tristan leaned on the last word as if exhausted by the very idea.

"Did you see the ghost?"

"No, but Dad did. He didn't tell me about it, but I heard him on the phone, talking to my uncle. He said he was really freaked but didn't want to leave because I was having fun and he didn't want to scare me. I asked him about it, but he didn't answer me. He said he'd been imagining things or that he'd probably seen someone from one of the other shacks. But that wasn't true. I think he really saw the ghost."

"Huh," Dez said.

"Do you believe in ghosts?" Tristan asked.

Dez peered down at the kid, wondering how best to answer. Dez didn't just believe in ghosts, he *knew* they were real. Knew firsthand.

No way to avoid it when your brother possessed the unusual skill of seeing the spirits of homicide victims.

Sullivan "Sully" Gray stretched out on the unmade sofa bed and unfolded Emily Crichton's paper to scan the section of the front page beneath the fold.

She always read her paper first thing, insisting on waking shortly before five so she had her coffee on by the time the newspaper dropped outside her apartment door. Many mornings, by the time Sully woke up, Emily had finished with it and had slipped it beneath his door for him to read.

Given the rough path of his life, there was comfort to be had in normalcy, in being able to sit down to do the morning crossword while, on the other side of the small bachelor suite, the coffee machine dripped out the morning supply.

Late winter and the sun seemed a bit sluggish today, so Sully held the paper closer to the lamp to scan the headlines.

Protest impedes Dead Man's Lake development

The past few years hadn't been conducive to staying up to date with the news, so the headline had Sully scanning the article for information on the proposed development. Dead Man's Lake had been one of his dad's favourite summer fishing spots. There was one small bay in particular Flynn Braddock had enjoyed dropping the anchor, one he had self-dubbed Trout Haven. Sully could still picture Flynn, grinning widely as he urged Dez or Sully to take his photo so Mara could see him holding his latest catch.

The memory put a smile on Sully's face—one the article quickly wiped away. A company called Bright Sands was looking to develop a large section of the lakefront for use as a resort community. It had been petitioning the government—the current land holder—to grant the purchase, but had run up against roadblocks in the form of protesters. Not everyone, it seemed, was eager to see a large swath of forest removed and a bunch of lakeside mansions erected in their place.

Sully fully understood their opposition.

He was interrupted mid-grumble by his cellphone, ringing from its spot on the end table. He reached over to snag it from its charging cable and recognized Dez's number on the display.

"Did you read the paper this morning?" Sully asked by way of greeting.

"No. Why?"

"The proposed Dead Man's Lake development."

"Oh, that. Didn't you hear about it before?"

"I don't stay in the loop as much as I should, I guess." It was true. Filled as his life was with tragedy and pain, many days he avoided the news altogether. Sometimes, all he'd do was scan the paper's headlines. Other times, he'd flip right to the puzzles and comics, then dump the paper in the recycling bin.

"Well, it's been an ongoing battle," Dez said. "So far, the development company's grabbing the short straw. It's an election year and there's enough opposition to the proposal to keep the government dancing around that one. I think they want the money. They just don't want to lose control in the process."

"Isn't there supposed to be some sort of public consultation process over things like this?"

"Not really. I mean, it's government land but it's not a park or anything. They can sell off Crown land as long as no one's renting it or holds some other sort of rights. But so far, people have been pretty vocal about not wanting development there. There have been a lot of calls for a public consultation process, so fingers crossed."

"Yeah, fingers crossed." It occurred to Sully Dez had likely called for a reason. "So what's up? Lachlan didn't cancel out on his share of surveillance duty this morning, did he?"

"No, nothing like that. Something else kind of interesting came up, and I wondered whether it might be our kind of problem."

"I hate to ask."

Dez provided the info anyway. "One of Kayleigh's friends came over this morning. He said his dad saw a ghost while they were ice fishing at Dead Man's Lake this weekend. He thinks it's *the* ghost."

"The Ice Man?" Sully asked. "I didn't think there was anything to that. Just a lot of tall tales."

"Apparently it's a little more than that," Dez said. "I know the kid's dad. They live down the block. He's a solid guy, not prone to making things up. But there's something else too. Tristan told me he caught something that really freaked his dad out: a piece of fabric. It got me thinking. What if this Ice Man story's true? What if what Tristan caught is evidence the ghost is real and his body's in that water somewhere?"

Sully smiled knowingly into his phone. "You're hoping to get out of the surveillance gig, aren't you?"

"Shut up. I'm serious."

"Since when have you ever purposefully tried to involve yourself in an investigation involving a ghost?"

"Since now. Look, Lachlan's got surveillance covered until after lunch. I'm going to head over to Adam's right away and ask him about what he saw. If it pans out, I thought maybe you and I could swing by Dead Man's Lake, check it out."

"You really are serious," Sully said. "Okay. Do you want me to come over and go with you to talk to Adam?"

"Nah. Knowing him, he'll have a hard enough time admitting it to *me*. If another guy's around, he'll probably deny everything."

"I hear you. Give me a call if you decide to head to the lake."

Dez disconnected, leaving Sully to stew over the article's contents. Reading down further, he read a quote from Bright Sands CEO, Clive Josprey, going on about the fact the development would bring many needed jobs to the area, both temporary and permanent. He had envisioned not just homes but an entire community. There would be stores, a gas station, a marina and restaurants. Some tourism-based businesses had also expressed interest, from a company specializing in speedboat tours and pontoon boat rentals to another wanting to set up an outdoor adventure park complete with zip line.

The idea of it made Sully's stomach turn.

He scrolled through his contacts, then tapped on the number he had for Paul Dunsmore. The son of former business magnates, Paul had liquified his assets before scandal surrounding his family's illegal doings broke Dunsmore Developments wide open. With shareholders—those who weren't tied up in the same scandal—fighting over the scraps of the company, Paul had taken his own sizeable portion and put it into helping the community. He was the driving force behind a handful of shelters as well as The Hub, an inner city community centre that acted as both soup kitchen and program space. Most recently, Paul had turned his attention to helping to fund a program intended to aid those trying to exit gang life.

Paul answered on the second ring. "Sully!" he exclaimed.

Sully grinned at the joy in the man's voice. "How are you, Paul?"

"Never better. I haven't felt more productive in my entire life."

"Getting out from under the thumb of your family was a good way to go, huh?"

"You said it. I mean, I've always tried to do the things I'm doing. It's just the first time I'm not faced with constant criticism from my family. They're playing it very low key these days, staying out of the public eye as much as possible." He laughed. "My father might actually come to me someday for advice."

"That he might," Sully said. "Hey, I was wondering. Have you been following this Dead Man's Lake development they've been talking about in the news?"

"I have. It's a shame, if you ask me. We're lucky to live in an area with so much pristine natural beauty. The first thing people like Josprey want to do is tear into it and tame it for human use. We just can't have anything nice, can we?"

"What are the chances of stopping someone like him?"

"Pretty good, I'd say. It's government land, and the last thing politicians want to do is piss off voters, especially during an election year. A couple of media outlets have done polls and they point overwhelmingly to an opposition to development at the lake. And the protest groups have grown quite a bit over the past year as Josprey and his minions have been trying to dig in their claws. Last protest about the proposed development had something like twelve hundred people present. That's a pretty sizeable number to show up for a protest over a proposed land sale.

"That said, sometimes money speaks louder than words. The government wants votes, but the state of the economy at the moment isn't great either. They'd definitely love the money that would come with a deal like this. Short-term pain could be long-term gain if those dollars are transferred into programs of benefit to large segments of society. It's all in the spin, you know."

"I didn't think of that. Maybe they'll agree to have public consultation on this."

"Maybe. Josprey won't be happy. There's a man who doesn't like to be questioned. Personable enough fellow on the surface, but he likes things his way. I can't imagine he's very happy with the audacity of the protest groups putting a damper on his plans.

But then, I guess you could say the same for most people in big business. When you've made plans to invest millions, you want things to go as smoothly as possible to maximize that investment. Hiccups in the plan can be far more than an inconvenience."

"Makes me even more grateful for the protestors."

Paul paused, and Sully could sense the question before it came.

"I'm curious," Paul said. "I know you and your brother go camping sometimes. Is that why you're so interested in the outcome at the lake?"

"Sort of." Sully glanced over to the kitchen as the coffee machine finished perking. He put the phone on speaker as he headed over and pulled a washed mug from the drying rack by the sink. "Dad, Dez and I used to go fishing there. It was Dad's favourite spot if he just wanted a quick day out on the lake. I have a lot of good memories there."

"And it makes it harder when those memories are about a person you can't make new memories with. I get it."

Sully poured out the coffee, then mopped up a small spill before carrying the mug carefully to the kitchen table. "That's a big part of it, I guess. A lot of the changes in my life over the past few years have been bad ones. I guess I've got to the point where I just don't trust change."

"You're an old man in a young man's body, my friend."

Sully took a cautious sip of coffee before deciding he'd have to wait for the heat to settle. "I've kind of always been an old man."

"Gift like you've got, I don't doubt it. Tell you what, I'll keep my ear to the ground on this proposed deal, see what shakes out. In the meantime, try not to worry about it. I've figured out the key to living my best life is to throw my energy and money into the things I can fix. Some things are out of our control, Sully. Once you learn to identify those things, the next step is teaching yourself how to let them go."

"Maybe that's my problem," Sully said. "My entire life has been filled with ghosts. When it comes to letting things go, they set really bad examples."

AFTERWORD

Thanks so much for reading. I am continuing to work on the next Dez and Sully books, and would be pleased to keep you updated on future projects and release dates if you would like to join my mailing list. As an added bonus, a growing anthology of short stories, entitled *Haunted: The Ghosts of Sullivan Gray*, is available as a gift to subscribers. Visit my website at hpbayne.com to sign up and grab the current version of *Haunted*.

The books in *The Braddock & Gray Case Files* are intended as standalone books, so they can be read independently of each other and from the preceding *The Sullivan Gray Series*. *Braddock & Gray* follows the events of *Sullivan Gray*, so those who have read the previous series will find a few cookies scattered here and there. I will include links below to the books in *The Sullivan Gray Series* should you wish to check them out (if you haven't already, of course).

The books in *The Sullivan Gray Series* can also be read as standalones to some extent, each containing a plot that wraps itself up by book's end. But there is a deeper plot that threads throughout the seven novels, so for that reason, I always suggest they're best read in the following order:

Black Candle

Harbinger

The Dule Tree

Crawl

Hollow Road

Second Son

Spirit Caller

As mentioned, the books in *The Braddock & Gray Case Files* can be read as standalone novels, but for those interested, here's the publishing order:

The Edge Creek Light

The Haunting of Thornview Hall

The Wynne Witch

The Blake Ghost

As always, I wanted to take a moment to thank my family and friends for their incredible support. I am so appreciative of all the people in my life who have been at my side throughout this journey.

A big, Dez-sized thanks also to my brilliant editor Hannah Sullivan and to my absolutely stellar team of advance readers, all of whom ensure each of the books is all it can be and more. And thank you as well to my subscribers and my followers on Facebook, especially the Sully's Spirits among you. I am incredibly grateful to you all.

And, of course, a huge thank you to everyone who's picked up this and other Sully books. I thank you from the bottom of my heart for making my author dreams come true.

ABOUT THE AUTHOR

Fascinated by ghost stories and crime fiction, H.P. has been writing both for well over two decades, drawing on more than fifteen years in a career in a criminal justice setting. Raised on a farm on the Canadian Prairies, H.P. enjoys reading, portrait drawing, travel and spending time with family and friends.

For more information, visit H.P.'s website at hpbayne.com.

ALSO BY H.P. BAYNE

Books in The Sullivan Gray Series (best read in the following order):

Black Candle

Harbinger

The Dule Tree

Crawl

Hollow Road

Second Son

Spirit Caller

Or pick up the box sets:

The Sullivan Gray Series Box Set 1

The Sullivan Gray Series Box Set 2

Books in The Braddock & Gray Case Files (can be read in order or as standalone novels):

The Edge Creek Light

The Haunting of Thornview Hall

The Wynne Witch

The Blake Ghost

Made in United States
Orlando, FL
05 August 2022

20588471R00086